THE DESCENT

THE OFFICIAL MOVIE NOVELIZATION

THE DESCENT

THE OFFICIAL MOVIE NOVELIZATION

by CHRISTIAN FRANCIS

based on the screenplay by NEIL MARSHALL

TITAN BOOKS

The Descent: The Official Movie Novelization
Print edition ISBN: 9781835414798
E-book edition ISBN: 9781835414804

Published by Titan Books
A division of Titan Publishing Group Ltd
144 Southwark Street, London SE1 0UP
www.titanbooks.com

First edition: October 2025
10 9 8 7 6 5 4 3 2 1

A CIP catalogue record for this title is available from the British Library.

EU RP (for authorities only)
eucomply OÜ, Pärnu mnt. 139b-14, 11317 Tallinn, Estonia
hello@eucompliancepartner.com, +3375690241

Designed and typeset in Hoefler Text by Richard Mason.

Printed and bound by CPI Group (UK) Ltd, Croydon, CR0 4YY.

Prologue

SUMMER 1939

The village of Heritage had been nestled on the southern edge of the Blue Ridge Mountains ever since settlers first made their homes across North Carolina. Looking to live in the solitude and peace of the Appalachians, they were uncaring about the indigenous land they stole, and despite battles, Heritage remained. With a population of fewer than a hundred souls, its community lived off the grid. Its fields yielded an abundance of crops: apples, peaches, and a variety of berries, all of which thrived in rich soil. Every season was marked by the rhythm of planting, growing, and harvesting. The village drew its water from clear springs, as the people passed their skills of hunting, fishing, and foraging down through the generations, ensuring no one went hungry. It was a place of the old ways, respecting the mountain they lived on. The high rocks sheltered the village from the world beyond.

"Freakin' yokels," Henry Sawyer grumbled as he got into his rusted pickup, slamming the door behind him.

Having had no choice but to stop in this small village

to ask for directions, he had been met with only vacant, unhelpful stares.

"They say where it is, boss?" a young voice from the driver's seat asked.

Sawyer turned to Ed Oswald, the newest mining crew member, who sat fresh-faced and smiling behind the steering wheel. Sawyer hated that he had to travel with this kid and resented his perpetual joy—a trait he wished he could punch right out of him.

"Kid," Sawyer said, "does my face look like I got the news I wanted? Am I smilin'? Do I look happy to you?"

Ed, barely nineteen, shrugged. "You look like you normally do, boss." He gulped. "I... I don't think I've ever seen you smile, if I'm speakin' plainly."

Unable to contain a sudden grin, Sawyer's rough beard parted, revealing a set of browning teeth behind cracked lips. "Well, you got me there. Let's just continue up the track a way. Gotta be along here somewhere."

"They didn't help us to the caves at all?"

"Nope." Sawyer shook his head. "And I told you already, stop callin' 'em caves. They're pits. Miners call 'em pits."

"Sorry, boss, I forgot."

The ride up the rocky track was precarious and slow going. Tools in the flatbed rattled loudly. Pickaxes, shovels, pans, hand-crank drills, sledgehammers, oil lamps, and a box of dynamite clanked and banged against the suspension of the old pickup.

As he drove, Ed didn't say a word and just stared ahead with immense concentration etched on his face. Not only desperate to get them there in one piece—if they could ever find it—he also wanted to impress Sawyer. He needed to keep this job.

Ed's uncle—one of the crew they were on their way to find—had vouched for his nephew to the company as a great driver and a hard worker. Something Ed knew was a big chance for him to be given. His uncle's reputation was in Ed's hands, and how he did was up to Sawyer.

Money was tight for Ed, of course. His family needed it. Since his father passed, Ed had been the sole breadwinner for his sisters and mother. He had to step up, and this job promised more income than he could have got lugging coal or rolling paper at the mill. No, this was a chance he wouldn't give up, nor one he would fail at. Too much was riding on it.

Sawyer, on the other hand, had no one to support, no family except the men on his crew, the men he knew and trusted. But he resented being stuck as the mentor to anyone this young. Not because he was a mean person, but because he had seen how new workers could end up. No matter how you teach someone to tie the rope or hold the pick, all new crew members were accident magnets.

Before Ed, in the last year alone, three new crewmen had been hired. Three young, happy, eager annoyances that all ended up the same: injured and having to quit. Mining wasn't a safe job, especially when mining old, uncharted underground systems. But no matter what, each new job started with a new man waiting to be mentored, and it was Sawyer's turn to teach him what to do so he didn't get killed.

After an hour of slow driving, as the winding dirt track snaked up even higher, they reached a plateau as the track veered left into a large swathe of woodland.

"We'll go as far as we can here or just make camp and walk it," Sawyer said. He glanced at the sun that had begun its descent towards the horizon. "Won't make it back down in the dark."

"Hey, look!" Ed pointed ahead of them.

Up ahead, the tree line parted, and a makeshift campsite emerged from between the trees. Three other rusted pickups had been parked on one side.

"Well, halle-fuckin'-lujah," Sawyer said.

The pickup rolled to a stop beside a small cluster of two-man tents sitting around a used firepit.

As Sawyer got out of the truck, he surveyed the site with a sense of unease. "Check those tents. I'll start unloadin'."

After closing the driver's door quietly, Ed obediently walked over to the tents. At each one, he unbuttoned the flaps and peered inside, expecting to find the crew asleep. But he found only empty cots.

As Sawyer carried a crate of pans from his pickup to where other tools had been left, he noticed the burnt-out fire in the centre of the camp. He moved over to it, crouched, then held his hand over the blackened wood. His weathered face creased with concern; the fire had been out for some time.

"This ain't right," he muttered, scanning the area.

"Nothin' in the tents over here," Ed said, walking to Sawyer. "Ya think they gotta be off down the pit?"

"Not now, no." Sawyer scrunched his brows. "We all start early and always end early. Always. No exceptions."

"How come?" Ed asked. "Not like you can see the daylight down there."

"'Cos pits change at night," Sawyer explained matter-of-factly. "Dunno how, but they always do. Like the dark outside brings new dangers down there. No digger stays past sundown. It's unspoken but always followed."

"Unless they found something good, I guess?" Ed added, hopeful.

Sawyer sighed. "Sure, I guess," he said, though he didn't believe a word.

In all his years as a digger for the Eastern Mining Corporation, he had never seen a big find on any of their scouting trips. Their job was to go around the country, finding cave systems that may still have some remnants of gold in them. And if they had them, they would call it in for a proper digging excavation.

The only issue was that most underground systems had been stripped bare decades before.

Finding a brand-new cave was rare. Finding one with an abundance of riches inside was even rarer. The most they could hope to find were small nuggets of gold they could excavate and bring in themselves. But these caves, though unofficially charted, must have been dug out.

As a crew, they had been scout-mining over the Appalachians for nearly a year. Each cave they were sent to was allegedly untapped. But every time, it had been stripped clean long ago. And this was the last section of caves they'd been hired to check out. For the whole year, the sum of their efforts was collapsed tunnels and broken bones. There was no gold. Just weakened caves that required extra care to traverse.

"What do we do now?" Ed asked.

"We wait."

The night brought with it a cold that made sleep difficult for Ed. With Sawyer in his tent, snoring loudly, Ed woke up after hours of frozen restlessness and decided to sit by the campfire.

None of their crew had returned in the hours since they made camp, and despite Sawyer's gruff insistence that all would be fine, Ed was still very worried. Intuition scraped his mind that something had gone wrong.

In the tent, still dressed in his dirty overalls, Sawyer was dreaming of what he always dreamt of: mining. It's all he knew and all he ever did. That, and drinking. He had no time for love, or travel, or family. He was content to dig until the day he keeled over dead. But tonight, his dreams were ripped away as a shattering cry ricocheted from outside.

"Help!" Ed screamed from the far side of the camp.

Sawyer lurched upward, violently awoken. Scrambling out of the tent, he struggled to focus in the darkness. As he tried to discern where the scream had come from, Ed appeared by the tree line holding a lit lantern.

"I need help!"

Rushing over, Sawyer saw what had caused Ed to yell

out. A man was slumped against a tree, broken, coughing up blood as he tried to breathe.

This man, dressed in torn overalls, was caked in blood, mud, and filth. His skin was stained by a murky redness. Ragged wounds marred his body—and deep gashes that oozed almost-black in a slow, pulsing rhythm. His breathing was shallow and hitched. His wide eyes were pale, terrified, catatonic, staring ahead at nothing, glazed over with shock.

Despite the state of this man, Sawyer recognised him easily. Chuck Barnecki. The crew's pit leader.

"Chuck, what happened?" Sawyer said, and his voice shook as he crouched beside the man. "Where's everyone?"

Ed couldn't contain his panicked tears. He had never seen injuries like this.

"Chuck!" Sawyer screamed louder.

But still no reply.

He noticed the gouge across the man's stomach, a wound so large and deep he could see his glistening intestines poking out.

Before anyone could retch at the grotesque sight, before anyone could run to find some help in the small village down the mountain, before Sawyer could reassure Ed that everything would be okay, Chuck spoke his final words.

"I left 'em down there," he spluttered as his face contorted in torment. "God forgive me. I left 'em. They screamed. They screamed so loud."

The light in Chuck's eyes flickered as he took his last ragged breath.

Sawyer stared down at his lifeless body.

"No, no, no," Ed wailed. "This can't be happening."

Sawyer couldn't allow Ed to be consumed by his fear. He had to find his crew, and he needed Ed's help to do it.

Following a blood trail that Chuck had left in his injured wake, the search for the pit proved easy. A hundred yards from the campsite, a large hole opened wide at the base of a high rock face, giving way to a dark cave system below.

A series of ropes crawled out from the darkness and led to a set of iron pitons that had been hammered into the dirt. Each rope that trailed downward had been knotted around its own piton.

Ed stood behind Sawyer, barely able to talk. Images of Chuck spun in his head like a nightmarish carousel.

Sawyer stared down at the ropes with grim resolve. Carrying his hard hat in one hand, a pickaxe in the other, and a lit oil lamp hanging from his belt, he spoke without turning to Ed. "You wanna help your uncle, right? No time to cry or be scared. You got me? Especially down there. That asshole, Chuck, must've left them trapped." He gritted his teeth. "We never leave anyone. Ever."

"But what did that to him?" Ed bawled, unable to control his emotions. "His belly... It was—"

"I told you pits ain't good after sundown."

He stepped forward, the cave's entrance opening in front of him. He knew full well that night was still very much upon them, and that any danger he spoke of was still very much present.

"If ya finished your tears, grab any rope ya want," Sawyer

said, motioning to the ones fixed to the pitons. "You know what to do... you've done it before. And don't think of Chuck. Just think of your uncle waitin' for us down there. How happy he'll be that we came after him."

It was the smell that hit them first: a mix of decay, damp earth, and something more pungent. Something that clawed at their instincts, telling them to turn and run. But Sawyer, wearing his miner's helmet—complete with his name painted in large black letters on the front—ignored the smell, tightened his grip on the rope, and descended into the void. The oil lamp attached to his belt swung with each movement, its beam doing little to break through the gloom.

Ed descended slowly on the left just behind Sawyer. His hands trembled as he used all his strength to hold his weight. His helmet—also with his name painted on the front—was slightly too big for his head, and it moved about precariously.

The coil of rope Sawyer had made him carry over his shoulder dug into his neck and restricted his movement, but he was happy not to be the one carrying the heavy pickaxe. The lower he went, the more Ed tried to control his breathing. Fear spiked his breath with every exhalation as every fibre of his being screamed at him to run.

He just wanted to go home, but he had no choice, and his uncle could be in danger.

The air around them grew colder the deeper they descended, and the ambient hum of nature became more and more distant, replaced by a hollow echo of emptiness.

The rope ran out just as Sawyer hit the floor, and a crunch came from under his boot. The moonlight barely touched them, but as he angled his oil lamp down, its glare exposed the small remains of animals strewn across the rocky surface.

He grabbed the large pickaxe from his belt and white-knuckled it.

"Fast and quiet," Sawyer said in a low rasp, once Ed reached the end of the rope beside him. "We find 'em and get the hell out, get me?"

Ed nodded. He straightened his hat, then adjusted the oil lamp on his belt. His pulse pounded with a rising panic and the rope slung over his shoulder felt heavier.

They moved cautiously through the small chamber, Sawyer in the lead. Ahead of them, the tunnel quickly narrowed into a jagged crevice, so much so that they had to duck through. The low ceiling scraped their backs.

Each sound made Ed pause. Every drip. Every crack. The deeper they travelled, the more noises they heard. His mind spun with all the possibilities of what lay ahead. For Sawyer, though, he knew that pits made all manner of noises. He had heard rocks groan and water cry. None of it fazed him, not anymore.

But the shuffling, wet scraping, like something dragged across the stones, made him freeze in his tracks. A sound directly ahead of them he had not heard before.

"What was that?" Ed whispered, voice barely audible.

"Shh," Sawyer hissed, his eyes scanning the weakly illuminated passage ahead.

After a few seconds the noise stopped, leaving only their heavy breathing and distantly dripping water.

Sawyer dismissed the sound and took a cautious step forward, testing each rock beneath his feet before shifting his weight. Ed followed, his heart pounding like a sledgehammer.

Then they came upon it—a deeper cavern. The tunnel in front of them opened, revealing a large domed space, the ceiling of which was lost in the shadows above. The walls around them were slick with moisture and shimmered in the light.

The air here was thicker and more difficult to breathe. Every inhale left a tangy, coppery taste in both of their mouths.

Still leading, aiming his lantern ahead, Sawyer crossed the cavern. Approaching the centre of it, he looked down, his oil lamp illuminating a yawning black void in front of them.

Frayed ends of ropes had been spiked at the edge of the hole with pitons, just like up on the surface, and each trailed down into the murkiness below.

"There," Sawyer said, pointing out the ropes to Ed.

But before they could follow their crew, a low, guttural growl reverberated behind them.

Sawyer froze, his hand tightening around his pickaxe. He forced himself to breathe steadily, keeping his eyes locked on the darkness ahead. This was more than just a normal sound from a pit. With a finger to his lips, he motioned for Ed to stay quiet, the urgency in his gesture unmistakable.

But there was no time to do anything else.

Out of the darkness, something barrelled towards them with terrifying speed. Sawyer barely had time to register the movement before an immense force slammed into his chest, sending him backwards. The oil lamp slipped from his belt and clattered to the ground, its light flickering wildly before it died out.

The ground gave way beneath him as he tumbled backwards down into the hole, plummeting at full speed, the world spinning around him in a disorienting blur.

Sawyer's agonised scream was so loud he could not hear Ed's from above.

His body clipped the rocky wall again with a sickening crunch, the impact knocking the wind out of him. He tumbled and tumbled, then slammed into his landing. A squelch echoed in the pitch black as bones shattered. Blood burst from his mouth, forcing him to choke as his body flooded with agony.

Where he landed was consumed by a dense, inky darkness, along with pungent rot. It was so overpowering it filled the cavern like a thick, vomitus fog. It was so awful that Sawyer could barely stop himself from retching through the blood that choked his windpipe.

He tried to move, but every attempt he made sent fresh waves of pain through his broken body. He could feel his strength ebbing away as fast as his consciousness faded.

Desperately, he reached out with one trembling hand, searching for anything solid in this darkness. Something to hold on to. Instead, his fingers brushed against something cold and wet—something fleshy that lay beneath him.

Panic surged through him as he realised he hadn't collided with rock or earth. He had landed on something dead. Something freshly dead.

A growl echoed off the far wall. One that grew louder, closer. The air around him seemed to vibrate with this sickening, primal noise, drowning out his pained gurgles.

His heart pounded erratically, the pain in his chest becoming unbearable, but he still fought to stay conscious. He had to survive. He had to escape. But here and now, he could not do a thing except lie in a heap, broken and fading.

The last thing he heard before the darkness swallowed him whole was a terrifying, monstrous shriek directly over him as a clawed hand dug into his chest.

Chapter 1
THE END

"Lean in!" Juno Kaplan yelped as the Hypalon raft crested above the colliding waters of the River Tay rapids. She clutched the nearest grip as the raft's snubbed nose lifted and the icy torrent beneath catapulted the raft into the air. It crashed back down on the whitewater with a raucous splash, and Juno whooped.

Behind her, gripping their oars firmly, Sarah Carter and Beth O'Brien did not feel as victoriously feral as Juno. They were both leaning into the middle of the raft, ensuring they wouldn't capsize as they bounded over the wash.

They wore bright yellow lifejackets and crash helmets securely strapped to their heads as they traversed the last legs of the tumultuous river.

"Forward!" Juno screamed, grabbing her oar and beginning to row.

On this command, Sarah and Beth leaned back out over the side of the raft and rowed in sync.

"Drop!" Juno yelled as she glanced back at her friends. "Isn't this freaking awesome?!"

Her American drawl never failed to make Beth smirk. As the only American in the friend group, Juno often amused her British friends with her pronunciation and quirky Americanisms, and this latest exclamation was no different.

"It's totally tubular!" Juno added as she fist-pumped the air, oar in hand.

"Cowabunga, dude!" Beth shouted in reply, a wide Cheshire cat grin plastered over her face. Her RP accent made her words sound intentionally ridiculous.

Sarah just shook her head and held on to her grip as the raft edged up on one side, then fell again.

As the water dropped away, the boat lurched forward and it fell four feet to the water below. They moved at speed downstream as the waters grew more and more violent around them.

"Stay alert," Juno shouted, loving her leadership role. "Gonna get a bit wilder from here on."

Sarah stared at Beth, wide-eyed and confused. *Wilder?* she thought. *How could it get wilder?*

The choppy waters tossed them about to and fro. Their bodies were yanked hard. Like rag dolls, they fell up and down, side to side, holding on to their grips for dear life.

The current dragged the raft at a furious pace. When they did not need to hold on, each worked their oars together, guided by Juno's commands.

"Left back," "High side," "Lean in." No matter what was called back, Sarah and Beth followed.

They may have looked less than enthusiastic about what they were doing, but that was only in comparison to Juno's ebullience and overexcitement. Sarah and Beth loved this. They just had a hard time concealing their fear on this wild ride.

The waters churned and twisted them along. When the spume occasionally cleared, they could see the bottom through clear water. Large boulders lurked beneath the surface, each looking as if it were lying in wait to snag flesh or break bones. That is what Sarah thought to herself as she glanced over the side between her frantic oaring. These morbid thoughts were soon dragged away as she heard the sudden song.

"Come all ye young fellows who follow the sea," Beth sang at the top of her lungs, barely audible over the roar of the water. "Wey hey, blow the man down." She glanced at Sarah. "Come on. And pray, pay attention and listen to me."

"Give me some time to blow the man down," Sarah belted.

They merrily shouted this song as they rowed the rough waters ahead. Juno, though, was silent. Her excitement was dulled by the exclusion. She did not know that song and felt like a third wheel between Beth and Sarah, which was not anything new. Being the only American in the group often caused her to feel alienated, which she understood and never blamed anyone for but always tried to make up for.

As their song ended, Juno leapt at the chance. "Row, row, row your boat. Gently down the stream." She turned as she sang loudly to her friends.

"Yes!" Beth shouted back. "Merrily, merrily, merrily, merrily. Life is but a dream."

The three screaming this nursery rhyme was secondary to the bellowing roar of the river. The crashing and smashing waves violently exploded into each other, soaking them and the raft as they rowed over it.

Between the gusting wind that pushed them at an incredible pace and the relentless current that dragged them along, the raft careened round the twists of the river with little control as it entered the lower course.

As they floated onward, the rocks on either side of the riverbank loomed high, cutting out any battling autumnal winds. Within a few moments, they had gone from hurtling over a cacophony of waves to drifting on peaceful ripples of shallow waters.

They could not help but burst out laughing, their song giving way to giggles.

Sarah gripped her oar, basking in her adrenaline-fuelled glow. They all did, feeling like they'd just won a battle as dopamine rushed through them.

Juno had the largest grin of all, naturally, and she turned to Sarah and Beth while barely holding in her exhilaration. "You think it's over, don't you?"

"It isn't?" Beth asked as her smile faltered.

Juno nodded ahead of them. "Calm before the storm, babe!"

Sarah peered ahead, and just beyond this stretch of river, the waters grew choppy again. The noise was even more turbulent than before. "What is that?!" she shouted to Juno.

"That," Juno replied in a raised voice, "that is the meat grinder!"

Beth could not hold in her laughter. "Who names it that?"

"We can quit now if you want," Juno added. "It's the last part, but it's the most dangerous and the most fun. Trust me."

All three began to backpedal to slow the raft down.

"I don't know if I'm ready for this yet," Sarah called out as she felt a strong urge to quit. "Bit above my skill set."

Not giving them much more time to think, the strong current tugged them along harder and harder.

"Well?" Juno asked as the thunderous noise ahead heightened. "Last chance."

Sarah peered farther downstream and could make out figures standing on rocks just beyond the rough waters.

"They're watching you, Sarah," Juno said as she also noticed them. "Let's make 'em proud, eh?"

Even though she could not see their features, Sarah knew it was Paul. Her husband. Her perfect husband. And Jessica. Her daughter. Her perfect daughter. Never an argument between them. Never a harsh word was spoken from their lips. She often felt that her life was too ideal to be real.

"Sarah!" Beth shouted, grabbing her attention. "Whad'ya say?"

Juno turned expectantly to them.

"Fuck it!" Sarah said with a sudden bravado. "Let's do this!"

On a large flat rock overlooking the end section of the rapids, in front of the steps leading down to the car park, Paul Carter crouched next to his five-year-old daughter,

Jessica. Both were wrapped up in padded coats, woollen hats, and thick gloves. Though not winter, the chill was biting.

"Here comes Mummy," he said as he wrapped one arm around his daughter.

"Is that her there?" Jessica asked, pointing at the furthest point of the rapids.

"Yes, can you see her? She's the one at the back on the boat on the left-hand side."

Jessica jumped on the spot. "I can see her! It's Mummy!"

"Ladies," Juno said, "remember to hold tight and keep rowing, no matter what. Even if you feel like it's not doing nothing!"

"Alright?" Beth looked at Sarah.

"Alright!" Sarah replied, determined.

"All-fucking-right!" Juno repeated. "Come on now, row!"

All three quickly thrust their oars into the water and began to row the raft towards the edge, across the point of no return.

The current pulled hard at the raft. With a stomach-churning yank, they were dragged over the edge and into the fray.

There was no more controlling their fate. They were, at the behest of nature, just witnesses to the river's incredible power.

With one hand on a grip, Juno screamed for joy.

Sarah and Beth were both the same as they held on to their grips for dear life.

The crashing water threw them every which way as the boat seemed to twist beneath them, bouncing off rocks on their way down.

"Mummy, Mummy," Jessica cried out in happiness as she saw the raft enter the calm waters at the base of this "meat grinder".

All three on the raft held the same wide-eyed expression. Relief, excitement, hyper-focus, and joy collided to render them temporarily speechless.

Eventually, Juno giggled. "Wanna do it again?"

No one answered, but Beth just shook her head with a smile as they drifted across the calm basin.

"Mummy," Jessica cried out again.

Sarah smiled as she waved at her family, and all three in the raft began to paddle towards the shore.

"You did it!" Paul called out. "You did it!"

Juno, glowing with the thrill of it all, glanced back at Sarah. "That wasn't so bad, was it?" she said. "Admit it—I was right! This was awesome and not hard at all?"

"Piece of piss," Beth added.

Sarah burst into a sudden laugh. Even though this was an established course, a place where few were ever seriously injured, it still made her glad to be alive.

Juno had been right. This was fun. This was needed.

As the raft hit the riverbank, Juno stood and waved to Paul and Jessica.

"Shall we?" Beth asked Sarah in a whisper, nodding to Juno as she carefully got to her feet.

Sarah smiled with mischievous glee.

Trying not to lose their balance—but more importantly, trying not to alert Juno—both moved closer to the head of the raft.

Juno, meanwhile, was busy clowning around for Jessica's sake, standing on one foot to mock a ballerina pose and sticking her tongue out. She yelped in surprise as her friends pushed her over the side, and she fell headfirst into the shallow waters with a massive splash.

"You assholes!" she shouted.

Beth, Juno, and Paul could not help but laugh.

Jessica just looked up at her dad. "What's an assow?"

"It's a Mummy-and-Daddy word," Paul said, still laughing.

As Sarah stepped off the raft, Jessica ran over and threw her arms around her.

"Jessie-bear, are you proud of your mummy?" Sarah asked, kissing her daughter on the head.

Jessica just replied with a tighter hug.

Paul, meanwhile, walked over to the shoreline and offered a hand to Juno, who was still in the water, looking annoyed.

With a thankful nod, she reached out and grabbed Paul's hand. As she did, a pendant fell from around her neck and onto her exposed cleavage.

Paul glanced down at the shiny metal resting on her wet olive skin and could not hide his smile. Juno noticed the gaze, and with a brazenly seductive smirk, she tucked the pendant back into her vest.

As she dragged the raft onto the shore nearby, Beth could not help but notice their interaction.

Sarah, meanwhile, was busy looking up at the dark-grey clouds crawling overhead. "We're lucky we booked the early slot today. Looks like it's going to bucket it down, doesn't—"

A thunderous rumble sounded above them, and rain suddenly erupted from the sky in a torrent.

"You think it's gonna rain?" Juno asked her with a smile.

Jessica giggled as her father walked over to her.

"Jess," he said, holding his hand out, "come on, you're getting soaked. Let's get to the car."

"Where are you parked?" Sarah asked.

"Just down here." Paul held Jessica's hand and turned down the steps leading to the car park.

"I'll be there in a bit. Just gonna help with the raft," Sarah added.

"Why don't you just go on ahead?" Juno said. "Beth and I got this."

"You sure?" Sarah asked as she unstrapped her helmet, allowing her long blonde hair to fall and hit her shoulders.

"Yeah, we can finish up here," Beth confirmed. "You should go. No sense in all of us getting soaked! Get Jess in the warm!"

"We'll see you back at the hotel, okay?" Juno said.

"Thanks, guys, really. You're both awesome." Sarah smiled then turned, hurrying after her family down the steps. "Wait for me, guys!"

Juno peered up through the falling rain at dark clouds as another thunderclap rang out. "Couldn't have held off five more minutes, could ya?" she sighed.

Raindrops thudded onto the hollow raft as Beth watched Paul's car leave the small, gravel lot in the direction of much darker clouds.

"Juno?" Beth asked. She turned back to her friend, who was busy deflating the raft.

"Yeah?" Juno said without looking up.

Beth spoke with a polite tone that belied the language she used. "What the fuck was that shit?"

Immediately, Juno paused and peered at her, blinking rapidly. "What the what now?"

"That look?"

Juno's eyes widened for a split second. "You're gonna have to use your words more, Ms Bethany O'Brien. I have no damn idea what you're saying."

"With Paul." Beth crossed her arms as if to make a bigger point. "You gave him that fuck me stare you give all the blokes."

Juno shot Beth a frown. "Paul?" Her question came out as if the notion was the worst thing she could imagine. "Do you take me for someone who shops vanilla?"

Beth shrugged. Doubt quickly crept into her head. Paul and Juno? That's ludicrous.

Juno chuckled and turned her attention back to the raft. "You think what really floats my boat is a guy who wears loafers and has a nice short back and sides?" Before Beth could respond, she continued. "You don't know me that well, do you?" She chuckled again. "Paul? Paul? Are you kidding? Really?"

"You raise a good point there." Beth shook her head.

"But it looked like you were giving him that look you always give those poor bastards you're about to ruin. And if Sarah saw that, she'd probably break your—"

"Paul, though?"

The rain began to pelt down, ripping them away from their conversation.

"Quick, let's get this packed away," Juno said, shifting their attention to more important matters.

The storm intensified, and the rain fell in a continual torrent onto the car's windshield as it snaked through the wild moorland of Glenbuck Loch. The wipers furiously sped back and forth as they tried to clear Paul's vision, but it was a constant losing battle. As soon as the rain was wiped away, it immediately skewed his vision once more.

Beyond his concentration on the road, Paul's mind was elsewhere.

The thunk, thunk, thunk of the wipers, along with the drumming rain on the vehicle's chassis, filled the silence.

Sarah, noticing his distraction, reached over and touched his hand that rested on the steering wheel. As if shocked from a dream, Paul recoiled quickly before shaking his head with a smile.

"Oh, sorry," he said, reaching out to hold her hand. "Was a million miles away."

"Are you okay driving? I don't mind if you're tired. I'm still buzzing from the rafting. I can drive."

"I'm fine, I'm fine," he replied, forcing him back into the present. "You've had a busy day."

As the sun began to set, the rain battered the countryside endlessly. The moors to either side of them were barely discernible through the windows.

They were not alone on these winding roads, though, as overbright headlights from oncoming vehicles occasionally passed.

Jessica, playing in the back seat, fumbled with her doll as she accidentally dropped it down into the footwell.

"Oh, poops." Leaning forward, she stretched out her small hand to try and pick it up again. But her seat belt held her back. "Dad?"

Paul was familiar with this regular occurrence. Reaching his arm behind his seat, he blindly patted the floor in search of the fallen doll.

"Bit more, bit more!" Jessica said happily as she watched his hand reach like a claw grabber at a fairground.

When Paul's fingers touched the cotton of the doll's leg, he grabbed it and handed it to Jessica with a smile—all while keeping his eye on the road.

Thunk, thunk, thunk. The windscreen wipers continued to battle against the torrent, filling the car with their rhythmic soundtrack.

As a truck passed by with its headlights on full beam, the blinding glare caused Paul to wince. His face fell to a somewhat maudlin expression again as his mind crept back to other things.

"Paul?" Sarah asked. "Are you really okay? You seem a bit distant."

Thunk, thunk, thunk.

Paul squinted as he stared through the rain-slicked glass.

"Babe?" Sarah added pointedly.

With a thin, unconvincing smile, he glanced at Sarah. "Really, I'm fine. Stop worrying yourself."

A thunderous crunch echoed ahead of them and stole their attention back to the road. Through the blinding rain, a pair of bright beams pirouetted wildly. Another smash, then the beams multiplied and advanced towards them with a monstrous ferocity.

No one had time to register what was happening as a large van and a small car collided up ahead, both hurtling towards them.

As Sarah screamed, she instinctively turned back to Jessica.

Paul frantically yanked on the steering wheel, not knowing which way to go, just trying to miss the twirling headlights.

But it was too late.

Andrew Adams had left his workshop in Limmerhaugh a lot later than he normally would have. Having spent the best part of the afternoon looking for a few ratchet straps in his overly messy storage shed, he had finally given up the search. He resigned himself to the fact that the two dozen ten-foot scaffolding poles in the back of his van would have to be secured by a single rope and knot. Though not optimal and not legal, with the bad weather coming in strong, if he drove sensibly no one would notice the lack of safety with his load. He had to deliver them to a builder's yard in Parish Holm by six p.m. if he wanted to get paid. Because of that, he could not wait any longer.

As Andrew merged onto Moorland Road, the rain had become significantly heavier than he had expected, but that did not deter him. He had driven in much worse, with much bigger vehicles. In this small truck—one he barely fit in, with his large belly pressed against the steering wheel as his stocky arms gripped it tightly—he drove at a sensible speed.

He did not see the oncoming car clip the edge of the road as it carelessly sped around the corner in front of him. He did not see that car spin as the wheel buckled under itself.

The last thing Andrew knew before his world ended was that something collided with him like a freight train, just as the scaffolding poles in the bed of his truck snapped their weak restraint.

Like missiles, the scaffolding poles were launched from the crumpled frame of the truck and flew off in different directions. Most clattered onto the asphalt, creating an almighty cacophony.

But one of them did not.

One of them cut through the air and, as if with a marksman's precision, pierced the Volkswagen hatchback's windshield in its ill-fated path.

Sarah knew she had been screaming, but she could not hear it. All she could hear was the terrified cries of her daughter and husband in the seconds before she was knocked unconscious.

In those few heartbeats, she saw the scaffolding pole tear into the car as if it were warm butter. It ripped straight through the top half of Paul's face. His jaw jutted back and forth in a horrifically swift death twitch as blood gushed out from his grotesquely demolished mouth and ears, eyes and nose.

The pole buried through his head and into the seat behind him.

Sarah's last conscious thought, before the car's door bent inward and smashed her into darkness, was that the pole had gone through the seat and that Jessica's screaming had suddenly stopped dead.

Chapter 2

A NEW DARKNESS

"Happy fifth birthday!" Sarah said softly.

Her voice was filled with love as she placed the birthday cake in front of Jessica. The five candles upon it flickered brightly in the dim living room, casting a soft glow on her daughter's innocent face.

Everything here felt perfect. The curtains were drawn, the air warm, the scent of the freshly baked cake wafting through the room as a ballad played quietly from the kitchen radio behind them.

Jessica's wide eyes sparkled as she looked up at Sarah with a grin. "I love you so much, Mummy," she said.

"I love you too, Jessie-bear," Sarah replied, leaning down and kissing her daughter on the top of her head. "Now, blow them out and make a wish, but don't tell me, or they won't come true."

As Jessica leaned forward, about to blow out her candles, everything began to shift. The light dimmed, and an icy feeling crept over the room.

"Jessica?" Sarah said, losing her breath as she peered

around the shadows that blotted out her surroundings.

With a large breath, unaware of what was changing around her, Jessica quickly blew out her candles. And when she did, the room was filled with a deafening screech of twisting metal, shattering glass, and terrified screams.

Sarah's eyes snapped open where she lay on the hospital bed, pulled into this unwelcome consciousness with a nightmarish bang. The sounds of her daughter and the sounds of the crash vanished as multiple monitors beeped rhythmically around her.

"Jessica..." she whispered weakly, the name barely able to escape her lips.

Lying in pristine white sheets, with multiple cables coming off various intravenous drips and electrodes over her body, Sarah stared wide-eyed up at the ceiling.

Her once-pale skin was littered with bruises and swelling.

She didn't jump.

She didn't scream.

She just stared at the starkness. Her mind reeled as it struggled to focus on what had happened.

Aching, she turned her head to one side. The pain of this movement caused her to let out a long sigh.

The monitor bleeped with every beat of her heart, coupled with a small light that flashed orange.

She tried to focus on it, but her mind was in a fog and her head pounded.

When she looked the other way, it was even more

painful. Her neck strained as she stared at the other bedside machines. But unlike the heart monitor, she had no idea what these were. Each displayed different numbers, and each beeped and whirred.

The confusion in Sarah's mind swirled. She forced herself to sit up, and a bolt of agony shot from her hip and traced up her spine. Despite this, she remained determined. She knew she had to move, even if she had no idea why.

Grabbing at a handful of cables that ran off from her body, she yanked them as hard as she could. If her body was not already ringing with extreme pain, she might have felt the needle tearing out of her arm and the blood dribbling from the opened puncture wound. But such pain was minuscule compared to the thunderous suffering gripping her whole body.

As she pulled at the remaining collection of wires, most just peeled off. More cables were yanked from her body when she swung her legs over the bedside and staggered to her feet.

Sarah opened the door to her room and peered out into the overly fluorescent hospital corridor, but she could not see anyone else. Tears streamed down her face with each step.

The lights flickered. One second, they were harsh and unnaturally bright, and the next, the corridor was cast into darkness.

Sarah staggered from her room out into the middle of the corridor, one arm cradled across her stomach since it was too painful to fully extend.

With a loud buzz, the furthest fluorescent strip of light

flickered and died, casting the far section of the corridor into a void.

When she was about to turn away, a noise from this new darkness caught her attention.

A scratching sound. Faint, but there. Angling her ear to the darkness, she concentrated. She could swear that it was not just scratching she could hear but also breathing—maybe her own?

The next light at the far end of the corridor abruptly cut off with a loud fizz of electrical static.

Her curiosity morphed into a feeling of danger. Sarah slowly backed away as the next light flickered out.

It was as if the darkness was following her as the fourth light in the row flickered and then cut out, casting the next section into pitch blackness. A pitch blackness that got nearer and nearer.

Sarah backed away. Another light cut out.

As she turned, the scratching and the breathing grew louder.

The fifth and then sixth sections of the corridor were cast into the dark in quick succession. Crawling towards Sarah faster and faster.

Sarah screamed in pain as she pushed her broken body into as fast a run as she could manage. But no matter her speed, the darkness closed in, each light dying faster than the last.

Sarah soon reached the end of the corridor. No exit. Just a blank, solid wall. An end to any escape. Before she could turn back and run into one of the rooms a few feet away, she became stuck in what was now the last bit of light. The only light in the corridor hung overhead.

It began to flicker.

"No," she whimpered as the bulb above her sparked and cut out, and with it, all the light was gone.

In a total darkness, she froze on the spot.

The pain in her pulsed. Her breathing hurt. Everything hurt.

The breathing was getting closer.

The scratching was getting louder.

The guttural breathing deepened as it took a sharp intake of breath, and a harsh rasping roar bellowed out—no more than a foot in front of her.

Sarah could only scream one painful word. "Jessica!"

"Sarah!" Beth cried out as she ran up to her in the hospital corridor. She stood, crying, just a few feet outside her room.

The hospital corridor was filled with sunlight through various windows. No harsh flickering fluorescence. No monstrous blackness.

All down the long passage, doctors and nurses milled around, paying attention only to their busy workload. Not one had noticed Sarah stepping out of her room and bursting into a flood of tears.

"Jessica," she blubbed as her legs buckled.

Beth caught her weight and held her as close as she could in a tight embrace. "I'm so sorry they're gone," she whispered. Tears choked her words. "But you're still here. You have to live. For them. You have to be strong."

Her words went unheard, though, as Sarah was trapped in her grief and unable to fathom this new and painful reality. She clung to her friend while they both wept.

Sarah closed her eyes, shutting out everything as her body went limp, and Beth's grip on her failed. Slipping to the floor, Sarah curled up in a ball.

"Doctor?" Beth called out in panic. "Please, someone help!"

Three weeks later

Beth stood alone in the hospital corridor outside Sarah's room. With her arms tightly crossed, she gazed through the small glass window at the space inside. There, lying on the bed in the middle of a very troubled sleep, pale and twitching, was Sarah. Her wounds and bruising had faded slightly, and she had begun to look more like herself.

Dreading this day, Beth felt scared. Scared at the thought of taking Sarah from the hospital—back into a world she no longer knew—and it was a terrifying prospect. But she couldn't abandon her best friend in her time of need. Not when she had no one else. No parents, no family... No family.

She wouldn't ever abandon her. Ever. Even if it was something she felt quite ill-equipped to manage. She had to at least try.

"Ms O'Brien?" Dr Morton called out, a gaunt man in his late fifties with silver-streaked hair and a lined face that wore the weight of a thousand difficult conversations. "I'm glad you're still here," he said, walking over.

"So, I can take her?" Beth asked quietly.

Dr Morton nodded. "Ms O'Brien, we have confirmed what you told us about Ms Carter's lack of support structure."

"Mrs," Beth corrected with a sharpness. "She would want to still be a Mrs."

With an accepting nod, the doctor continued. "Mrs Carter... I have spoken with social services in this case, as she does not have any next of kin. We can release her today under your care, provided you can assure us that her immediate medical needs are met. As long as you can supervise her for the next two weeks, there is no problem. We would normally—if someone has no next of kin—keep them admitted." He took a deep breath. "This kind of emotional trauma can cause patients to shut themselves off emotionally, physically, and mentally. Her instinct will be to retreat into her grief. So, you will need to ensure that you can be resilient against such reactions."

"Resilient? How?" Beth asked, looking back inside the room.

"If I am honest, she will probably hate you for a while."

The doctor's words stole Beth's attention.

"Hate? Me? Why?"

"It's only natural—and not always the case. But you should expect it nonetheless. Those who care for the grieving are almost always pushed away at first. Mainly since the patient suffering the loss will blame the world and feel like everyone else is forcing them to forget, to move on, before they are ready. But if this happens, and you feel it is too much, we can always have social services—"

"I won't let her go through this alone."

Dr Morton paused. "As long as you remember that there is help, should you need it." His tone was gentle, but his eyes were unwavering in their seriousness. "Recovering from her injuries... will be hard. Physically, Mrs Carter has a shorter road. A couple of fractures, bruising, nothing more. But what will be harder is her grief. It's not something you can simply 'get over'." He paused, letting the gravity of his words sink in. "My words of wisdom, for what they are worth to you, is that few people manage to fully recover from this kind of loss. So, please, try not to manage it on your own—for your sake. It can take a toll on those closest to the grieving. And you are not legally obliged to do any more than you wish. Rally her friends, try to provide a distraction for as long as she stays with you. But you will need to remember that this is her grief. Not yours. So, when her course of medication ends in fourteen days, she can go home unsupervised to process what she needs to alone. Check in on her as much as you wish. Just do the best you can to offer a new stable normality."

Beth's brow furrowed. She hadn't wanted to think about the emotional toll—the gaping hole Sarah's loss would leave behind.

"What's a stable normality?" she asked, her voice barely above a whisper.

"That is something I cannot answer," the doctor said. "It is different for each person, how they accept what has happened. The loss never really goes away. It will become like a second shadow—as in, it will always be there. At first, it may feel suffocating for her, just like it has been these past few weeks. And everything will feel overbearing. Everything she will do will remind her of those who are gone. It is another reason we try to ensure they do not go home until the behavioural medication course has had time to start working. But in time..." He chose his next words carefully. "In time, she will learn to accept. She will carry the loss like a new part of her. She will learn to remember without the hurt. And I say this as someone who has been in both your position and hers."

Beth wanted to say something, but her mind was too overwhelmed.

"So, we will release her to you after her lunch this afternoon. We have the address she shall be staying at?"

Beth nodded. "She's going to stay at mine for the rest of the month. Till after the funerals. I took time off work."

"Good. There will be some follow-up appointments we have booked for her, if you could try to ensure her attendance. They are a couple of physical therapy sessions and a counselling one. I have all the dates for you here." He pulled out a letter from his white coat and handed it to her.

Exhaling, Beth took the envelope. "Okay."

Dr Morton gave a sympathetic smile. "I wish you both well."

With a final nod, he turned to walk away, leaving Beth standing in the corridor, alone again.

Chapter 3

THE CABIN

One year later

The Jeep's engine hummed as it wound its way along a small road that fed off from Route 40, cutting through the state of North Carolina. The ribbon of asphalt snaked through the tree-covered northern Appalachian Mountain range. The towering peaks that loomed on either side of the road were shrouded in a thick autumnal mist rolling down its slopes like a slow-moving river.

The leaves had begun to turn, painting the thick surrounding woodland in brilliant shades of amber, gold, and red. The air was cool, crisp, and—since the heavy rains had stopped for a few days—carried with it a faint, earthy scent of pine mixed with wet leaves. In the dimming twilight, the landscape was almost magical.

Gripping the steering wheel of the hired vehicle, Beth swallowed forcefully to pop her ears. As the car drove up the winding road through dense forest, she had not really noticed their steady ascension to a higher altitude.

She'd been busy paying attention to the road ahead, which shrunk narrower and narrower. The farther she drove, the more the trees crowded in, drooping closer and closer to the vehicle's roof, entwining with other branches to block out most of the setting sun's rays.

In the passenger seat, Sarah peered out the window with a blank expression. Watching the trees pass, she was not really taking much of it in. Her hair had been cut much shorter. She had also lost weight she did not need to lose, giving her a gaunt appearance.

The Jeep's radio, which had been emanating Sixties rock'n'roll for the past few hours, began to crackle as it lost the station's signal. Soon, country music broke through the white noise.

"Dammit," Beth chided. Her free hand shot out and grabbed the radio's tuner. Turning the dial, she searched for any other available stations.

Through warbling static, swampy, twangy music broke the noise.

"Okay, so, we have either this mud, blood, and beer music or..." She twisted the dial again. Bellows of a Baptist preacher rang out of the speakers, condemning the modern world, threatening fire and brimstone to all the non-believers. "Or we have Mr Happy here." With an exhalation of annoyance, Beth chose instead to switch off the radio.

"We must be nearly there now, right?" Sarah asked.

Beth shrugged. "We passed that town, Heritage, a mile or so back. So, yeah, can't be that far."

With the road ahead getting darker from the thick

surrounding foliage, Beth squinted at the shadows shrouding their journey. She quickly switched on the headlights. The brilliance of the Jeep's lights flooded the road in front of them.

Then, as if from nowhere, a low-hanging branch came into view and banged against the car's windscreen, startling them both.

"Shitting hell!" Beth exclaimed. She shot a worried look to Sarah, knowing full well that, after what she'd experienced, a loud bang could be a trigger. "Sorry, I didn't see it. You okay?"

"Not your fault," Sarah replied as she tried to catch her breath through half-gritted teeth. The noise set her heartbeat racing. "Bloody trees."

Beth knew Sarah did not want to be on this trip, and that the only reason Sarah came was due to Beth's nonstop badgering. And she felt responsible for making sure Sarah had the best time. The best time away from her life. Her mind. Her memories. But she felt so guilty for dragging her this far.

"We don't have to do this, you know, if you would rather just be you and me," Beth said quietly. "We can turn back, stay in town, get wasted, and go to a barn dance or something. Don't care how close we are to the cabin."

"Barn dance?" Sarah grinned. "Not with your dancing—that's a frightening thought."

"Hey, I can dance like a bloody diva!"

Sarah just stared at her, holding back laughter.

"Okay, I can sort of dance."

Sarah raised her eyebrows.

"Fine, I'm a liability on the dance floor." Beth shook her head. "You happy?"

"Very, my two-left-footed friend." Sarah laughed.

Ahead, the Jeep's headlights illuminated a large sign on the roadside that boldly stated Chattooga National Park. Above the lettering was a side profile image of a stag, which had real bullet holes shot through the wood it had been printed on.

As they passed, Beth stared at the sign with wide eyes. "There were actual bullet holes in that sign, weren't there? You see that?" she said under her breath. "This may be my kind of place!"

Sarah sat up straighter in her seat. She turned to Beth, sensing her discomfort. "Hey, you know what? You're right. We don't have to be here. We could stay in town. And I could watch you drunkenly flail across a barn dance, hurting everyone in your wake. But I'm not gonna be the one to tell Juno that we bailed on her plans... Do you want to be the one to do that? You want to be the one in her firing line?"

Beth smiled. "Ah, yes. Of course. Juno. Always dragging us out to the middle of"—she gesticulated outside—"this."

"I know, right? To a beautiful vista," Sarah mocked. "What a fucking bitch."

"You know, she probably bribed someone to get our visas approved just so we had no reason not to come out. She finally got her way. The gang in the US of bloody A, on her turf for once."

"She's come over to see us enough times. She came to

England last year and the year before. And the year before that. Kinda our turn to trek around the world, isn't it?"

"Yeah, right," Beth muttered. "She came over last year, then left in a damn hurry when things got bad."

"Beth... that's no one's fault," Sarah said. "Love each day, right?"

"Huh? What does that mean?"

"Just something Paul used to say. Love each day. I used to think that was weird hippie stuff." She turned with a smile that covered an obvious well of deep emotion. "I understand what he meant by that now—love each day."

"I get it." Beth nodded. "Great motto."

"We know if Rebecca and Sam are there already?" Sarah asked, steering the conversation away from any more sadness.

"Well, they didn't have to contend with a delayed flight and a night in a flea pit motel, waiting for a car rental to show up, so they better be."

As the last light of day eked over the Appalachians and the moon began its ascent into a dark cloudy sky, the Jeep pulled up outside a small lodge nestled against a thick tree line that led up the mountain.

From the small windows, a warming orange light radiated out from within, and a familiar face peered out from the kitchen: Juno, with a big, excitable smile.

Just as the car's engine switched off, the door to the lodge swung open and Juno raced out onto the veranda to welcome them.

"Sarah, Beth!" Radiant and confident as ever, she stepped onto the gravel and raced over to the Jeep.

Beth waved with a smile. "Hey, Juno." She walked around to the back and opened its rear door.

"How you doing, Beth?"

"Sick of travelling. You?" Beth reached into the Jeep and pulled out her rucksack.

There were no hugs of welcome between them. A polite respect, but that was it.

Yet, as Sarah stepped out of the Jeep, Juno flung her arms around her before she even had a chance to get her bag.

"Sarah, doll face!" she exclaimed as she hugged Sarah far too tightly.

Pulling away, Juno then took Sarah's hand in hers and gazed into her eyes intensely. "Everything's going to be fine, you know?" Juno's words were almost patronising, unintentionally so. "Better than fine. It's going to be great! You need this, and I will provide."

Sarah just smiled, not taking any offence. "Hello, Juno."

"The others here yet?" Beth called out.

"Yeah, inside. They can't wait to see you both, but they may have cracked open the wine already," Juno said, then turned to Sarah. "Go inside. I got your bag."

With a smile of thanks, knowing that saying no would offend, Sarah walked up the step and into the cabin.

At the Jeep, Juno turned to Beth and spoke in a whisper, making sure Sarah was out of earshot. "How is she? All good?"

"Small moves, Juno. Small moves."

"Of course."

"She's here, isn't she? Let's count that as a big win. Just take the rest one step at a time." She walked towards the cabin. "So, don't worry, I'll look after her, just like always."

Juno sighed. "It's not a competition, Beth."

Not rising to the comment, Beth walked into the cabin without another word.

A log fire burned brightly at one end of the cabin's large open-plan room. A hallway branched off from one side, leading to each ensuite double bedroom. A simple yet cosy place.

Rebecca Van Ney, the tallest of the friends by quite a few inches, rose to her feet from her place in front of the fire. She rushed over to greet Sarah, who stood by the dining table looking exhausted.

"It's so good to see you!" Rebecca exclaimed, hugging her as enthusiastically as Juno had.

Without having a chance to reply, Sarah just hugged back. It was clear that all the commotion and attention was too much for her, yet she tried her best to hide it.

"Sarah!" another voice rang out.

This time, it was Sam Van Ney, Rebecca's younger sister and a smaller version of her, who spoke joyously as she stepped into the living room.

"Hiya, Sam!" Sarah replied. "Or is it Dr Sam now?"

Rebecca smiled and made way for Sam to run in for a hug.

"Not yet a doctor," Sam said. "Two more years to go."

"Only two?! Please tell me it's longer, the world isn't

ready for you to wield a scalpel," Beth said with a mocking look of despair. She put her bag down by the door.

Sam smiled. "I can treat your arthritis now if you like, Beth dear. I hear it all starts falling apart past twenty-five."

Letting out a loud guffaw, Beth slumped into a wooden chair by the dining table. "Is this what they teach you in medical school? How to take the piss?"

"Yes, they do!" Sam beamed. "I excel at it."

Last through the front door, Juno stared at Beth, looking annoyed, before she placed Sarah's bag down by the counter.

"Hey, Doc," Sarah said softly, still hugging Sam. "Thanks for your letter. It meant a lot, you know?"

"Sorry I couldn't be there," Sam replied.

"I was out of it most of the time," Sarah said. "But from what I do remember... you didn't miss much."

"I'm going to fix us some drinks," Juno said.

"I'll give you a hand." Sarah broke away from Sam and walked back over to the kitchen area, where the bottles of beer and wine sat on the counter.

From the hallway, Holly walked in. A young woman of nineteen, she was dressed in skate clothes and covered in multiple piercings, with short, spiky hair. A rolled, unlit cigarette hung from her lips.

Staring, Beth blurted, "You've got to be fucking kidding. How old are you?"

Holly walked over with a smile. "Pleased to meet you, too." Her Irish accent was thick. "You're the middle-aged teacher, right?"

“Damn.” Beth laughed. “Just put me in a rocking chair and pull the blanket over my knees.”

“This is Holly,” Rebecca said. “Juno’s... protégé? Assistant?”

“Eye candy,” Holly corrected.

“I thought Juno ate her young?” Beth retorted a bit louder than she had intended.

Rebecca and Sam laughed.

Juno tensed, facing away from Beth, as she opened a beer bottle.

Holly’s smile did not falter. “I’m a little bit tough for her to eat, I think.”

“I’ve heard all about you,” Sarah said before sipping from a wine glass. “You’re the crazy one who jumps off buildings, right?”

Holly laughed. “It’s called base jumping or parkour. It’s so much fun. You should try it.”

“D’you live in America?” Beth asked.

“Yeah, I ran out of things to jump off in Ireland. I’m on the lookout for the next big high.” She took out a lighter, lit her cigarette, and took a long drag.

Soon, everyone could smell it was not merely tobacco.

“I may want some of that,” Beth mumbled.

“I like your hair, Sarah,” Holly added, pointing to her own hair. “It’s better shorter, isn’t it?”

Sarah looked back quizzically.

“Juno showed me the photos of when you used to climb together,” Holly replied. “When you had long hair.”

Juno walked over and stood against the counter in

Sarah's eyeline. "Plus, I found this classic from our first ever trip. Here..." Juno took out an old Polaroid from her back pocket and handed it to Sarah.

It showed three teenage girls—Juno, Sarah, and Beth—with their arms around each other, elated, against the backdrop of a bright summer day. A trio of inseparable friends.

"Jesus!" Sarah exclaimed as she handed the photo to Beth. "Were we really that young?"

Beth peered at the photo and grimaced. "More to the point—was our hair really that shit?"

"Anyway, everyone?" Juno said. "Grab a bottle or a glass. We got wine, beer"—she motioned to Sam—"and gin for the doctor."

"Athankya." Sam mock curtseyed.

Juno raised her bottle. "Time to make a toast to a special someone."

Sarah's stomach dropped; she knew Juno was about to put more attention on her. "I'm just gonna go to the bathroom," she quickly said with a polite smile.

After she left the room, Beth shot Juno a stern look. "Cut it out. She's not ready for that shit!" she said in a whisper.

A whisper that Sarah heard as she walked down the hallway.

Juno rolled her eyes then took a swig of her beer.

Later that night, while the surrounding forest grew darker and more foreboding, the windows filled with condensation. The cabin itself had become louder with raucous laughter. The six women sat around the fire on the sofas, with Holly and Sam on a furry rug between them. On the two tables at the end of each sofa, multiple bottles of wine and beer stood empty. A testament to how the night had gone.

Sarah turned to Sam. "What happened to that Josh guy? Was that his name? The short one. You two still together?"

"Kind of, sort of." Sam shrugged as she gulped neat gin from her glass. "Different shifts mean different lives."

Sarah, recognising Sam did not want to talk more about it, turned her attention to Holly. "What about you? Any insignificant other? Or others?"

Holly laughed. "I'm like my girl Juno here, you know, into the sport of life. I'm not planning on doing anything that's not fun. But that's just for now."

"Oh?" Sarah asked.

"When I'm older, I wanna have lots of babies." Holly glanced at all the women in the room. "Anyone here wanna have kids?"

A sudden awkward silence filled the group. Rebecca grabbed Sarah's hand and squeezed it.

Beth looked shocked and shook her head.

"Oh, I'm sorry, Sarah," Juno said.

Noticing the reaction, Holly's face screwed up in confusion. "What? What I say?"

Taking a deep breath, Sarah managed a forced smile. "I had a daughter, Jessica. She was killed in a car accident last year."

Holly's stomach churned. "Aw, Jesus."

"But it's okay, though. I'm okay. I really am. You weren't

to know. And it's not like I wear it plastered on my forehead."

"Ah, shit, man," Holly said. "Juno told me about your husband, but I didn't—" She gritted her teeth and closed her eyes. "Fuck! I feel like a right twat." She glanced at Sarah again. "You can hit me if you want."

Unable to hold it in, Sarah let out a laugh. Totally uncontrolled. There was no obvious joke, but the awkwardness and strangeness of the whole situation simply became too much.

Holly stared in shock at Sarah's reaction.

"I'm sorry," Sarah said through her laughter. "I'm so sorry. I don't know why I'm laughing."

Slowly, everyone else smiled and laughed.

"So, is that a yes or no for hitting me? In the tits or face, I'm cool with either," Holly said, which sent the room into more hysterics. "I'm gonna like you all. I can just tell."

"Did I tell you Rebecca and I are going into business?" Juno said to Sarah, changing the subject. "We've set up a company and everything."

"Now that is funny," Beth added.

Rebecca laughed. "No, we really are."

"Seriously?" Beth said, her voice pitching high. "Seriously serious?"

"A company? Juno, isn't that a bit"—Sarah chose her words carefully—"conventional for you?"

"Sometimes, you just have to roll with it," Juno replied with a proud smile.

"Oh, I gotta hear more of this awesome idea." Beth leaned towards Rebecca.

The alcohol was making her tongue a bit too loose, so much so Juno could not miss her disdain.

"It's a woman-only outward-bound business," Rebecca said happily. "We're going to do trips all over the country. Climbing, caving, skydiving, surfing."

"A woman-only one?" Sarah asked.

Rebecca nodded. "Oh, there's a huge market for women who don't want the bullshit that comes with a mixed group."

"What bullshit?" Holly asked as she poured the dregs of the wine bottle into her half-full glass.

"Well," Juno said, keeping eye contact with Rebecca, "there's those gear freaks. You know, those guys who must have the latest gadgets and use them all the time. No room for instinct or expertise."

Laughing, Rebecca immediately could tell Juno's comments were directed jokingly at her. Then she turned to Holly to carry on the joke. "And the peak-baggers. They don't care where they are. It's just about whether they've got to the top of everything."

"Not gonna lie. They sound awesome." Holly smiled as she gulped her wine.

Sarah joined in and stared at Juno. "And the guys who've got to be the leader of every group, who've got to hold the map and turn the whole thing into an army exercise."

To which Juno gave a round of silent applause and mouthed the words very good to her.

Sam looked at Beth. "And the guys who make you the baby of the group even if you've done more than them."

"See?" Rebecca laughed. "You just don't get that bullshit with women."

Soon, as the laughter subsided and more glasses had been emptied, everyone decided it was time for bed. Before things got too drunken, they had to cut the festivities, since they had a big day ahead.

In one of the shared bedrooms, Rebecca padded around, preparing for the morning. She had just finished constructing her impeccably tidy pile of climbing gear at the foot of her bed. Everything was folded in a pristine manner, with every item piled in strict order of size. But at the foot of Juno's bed it was the exact opposite, a haphazard pile of crumpled clothes and gear left where they fell. On top lay an old dog-eared book, Caving in Chattooga.

Outside on the back porch, dressed in a long T-shirt with Kill the Hippies emblazoned across it, Holly leaned against the wooden railing overlooking the forest. Taking a drag on her joint, she closed her eyes, loving the feeling.

Next to her, also in her bedclothes, Sam drank from a hip flask.

"You go on these trips a lot? Together, I mean?" Holly asked. She handed the joint to Sam.

"I've only been on one. They've been doing it for years," Sam replied as she took the joint and passed the flask in return. "Juno started them when she was at school in England with Beth and Sarah. Rebecca joined when she met Juno."

"Do you find it weird to go on holiday with your sister?"

Holly swigged from the flask. Her eyes widened, having not realised what it was. "Whisky?" she asked, impressed.

Sam smiled and nodded. "And technically, Becca's my half-sister. Which means we see each other half as much as we should. And truth be told, we barely know each other."

"Oh, really?"

"Since she won't get involved in my world, it's up to me to get into hers, and I don't have a lot of time with med school."

"So, you're the sensible one of the family, then?" Holly laughed, and they swapped the flask and joint back over.

"Someone has to be."

Holly took another drag on her joint.

"You know anything about tomorrow?"

"About Boreham? Nope, as long as it's not like those other bloody tourist caves," Holly chuckled. Before Sam could say anything, she continued. "They're all like a goddamn Starbucks down there, you know—handrails and litter bins and what have you. It's a gross, sanitised excuse for a tourist trap masked as a 'climber's adventure'." She shook her head. "It's not in any way a fuckin' adventure, let me tell you that."

"So, what d'you want instead?" Sam asked.

"Excitement. The unknown. The walking on a knife's edge." Holly took another drag. "If you're a climber, jumper, caver, you have to just do it and not give a shite about what could be, or the thing that's bigger than you will get you in the end. And that's the excitement. So, I hope Juno's got something amazing lined up. Something bigger than us. Without fuckin' handrails. No idea about Boreham Caverns, though. Couldn't bring myself to look them up in case I got pissed off before I got there."

From the doorway, having overheard them from the shadows, Juno stepped onto the back porch. "I think what you're smoking might be bigger than you, Holly."

"Ah, you're no fun," Holly replied.

"You agree with Holly?" Sam asked Juno. "The more dangerous, the better?"

Juno took the flask from her hand. "It's not the sport that's dangerous—it's the people," she said after she took a sip, then handed it back. "Look at caves, for example. They're not waiting to hurt you as long as you know where you are. The lay of the land. Then you're fine if you got the skill or are led by someone who has the skill." She smiled smugly. "Like me."

Holly glanced at Sam, but it did not stop Juno from carrying on. "Look at Haverlock Caverns. Back in '88, ten guys went down there to see how deep they could go. They were all experienced, apparently. But they had no idea that a huge storm was about to hit. Some experts. And by the time they heard the rain pouring in behind them, they were already four kilometres down."

"And they drowned?" Sam asked.

Juno shrugged. "Well, they couldn't get back up through the water, so they went farther down to try and find some air pockets to ride it out. The lead guy somehow managed to squeeze himself through a tiny fissure in the rock ceiling. Enough for one person. But he was the only one who could fit in there. The rest were in the cave below, unable to do anything but wait." She paused. "He must have heard them screaming as they all drowned, trying desperately to get into that tiny space with him. When the rescuers arrived, they found his body covered in deep scratches where his friends had tried to claw their way into the fissure, hoping he'd save them. But there was nothing he could do. Only one person could fit in there. The doctors said that even if he hadn't died in a much more brutal way—which I'll get to in a minute—he would've bled out from those claw wounds in a matter of hours."

"Jesus," Sam exclaimed.

"He wasn't safe in that fissure, though. Well, only at first. You see, the water didn't just stop its flow below him—it kept rising. The pressure from four kilometres of water forced the rocks around him to crack and break inward onto him. He was wedged in tight, but the rising water squeezed him even tighter against the ceiling. Tighter and tighter. And the fissure he was in? Well, it wasn't just one small hidey-hole. It was a fissure that led to dozens of much smaller fissures along it. So, as the water rose, it cracked the ceiling further, pushing the rocks—and him—higher, squeezing him through those dozens of tiny fissures. Half of his body—the part closest to the ceiling—had been crushed and forced through that network of tiny cracks. His body was stuck, almost like the hair on a Mr Potato Head. So, when the water receded and the rescuers came in, they discovered his remains were stuck to the ceiling. Most of him had been pushed through into the dozen narrow cracks above. They had to slice him down. In the end, they could only bring a fraction of him back out. The rest of him had been squished into rock. No way to get that out so far down. So, the authorities closed the caves for good. Calling it all a graveyard."

"And how does this relate to anything whatsoever?" Holly asked.

"It had rained in the days before. There were heavy showers predicted. And the caves were already known to be prone to flooding." Juno took a breath. "My point is, the caves and the rain were not the real danger. Anyone with any experience should know to never go into caves that have ever flooded if there is rain anywhere near it. It's common sense. Especially in Portland, where rain is often heavy. And especially when going that deep. Every bit of research can save you. So, it wasn't the caves. It was the people."

"What would you have done, then?" Holly asked. "I mean, you think you would have done better down there?"

"I would have survived—I can tell you that." Juno smirked and walked back to the cabin door. "Now, get to bed. We got a long day ahead of us."

Feeling a chill, Holly quickly stubbed out her joint on the wooden beam and turned to follow Juno. "Come on, then, time for us to hit the hay," she said to Sam.

"She really had to tell that story before bed, didn't she?" Sam said, trailing her.

Holly turned with a giggle. "Hey, don't fret yourself. Super Juno will save us all, apparently."

*

Later that night, in the third bedroom of the pitch-black cabin, Beth was fast asleep, snoring lightly.

Sarah, meanwhile, was lying on top of her covers in a long white nightshirt. Her eyes were wide open, having been unable to find any sleep. She stared glassy-eyed at the ceiling.

With a frustrated expression, she rolled out of bed and got to her feet. Her bare skin ached from the cold wooden floorboards.

Over at the slightly ajar bedroom window, she moved the curtain to one side to let the cool night air hit her unobstructed. She took a few deep breaths in and stared out towards the dark tree line. With the silver moonlight breaking through the clouds above, the forest seemed to shimmer in a ghostly hue as the beams of light reflected off the dew coating the leaves.

But there was something else there.

A flash of yellow light.

Something.

Far into the woods. Like a flashlight pointed at her.

But it was getting closer.

Scanning the trees, she squinted as the light quickly disappeared.

She had half-convinced herself that she was imagining the light when it appeared again. This time, it was spinning as it got closer and closer.

Then came a sound from behind her. A giggle.

Losing her breath, Sarah looked over her shoulder into the dark room. Is there someone here?

A rhythmic pounding then began in her head. She peered out the window again. The light was flitting between the trees.

Then the giggle came again.

A child's giggle.

A young girl's giggle.

Her young girl's giggle.

No.

No.

Get a grip, Sarah.

Get. A. Grip.

Shutting her eyes tightly, she leaned forward and pressed her head firmly to the condensation-covered glass, hoping the cool moisture would somehow ease the ache in her mind. Somehow ease everything in her mind.

Before she had any time to react—

Smash.

A scaffolding pole burst through the window, impaling her skull, launching her body backwards onto the wall behind her. Her body was left hanging a foot off the floor as a torrent of blood spilled out of her mouth and down her nightshirt.

Chapter 4

THE SINKHOLE

Sarah's eyes shot open as she woke with a startle, covered head to toe in a sweaty sheen. She shot up in her bed. Slowly, she peered around the dark bedroom, half-expecting something to jump out at her. But nothing awful waited in these deep shadows. It was just the violent memories she couldn't shake from her mind painting her waking life. But as she sat in her bed, the darkness shielded the walls and made the room look like it stretched out forever.

"Jesus." She shivered, shaking off the memory of her nightmare.

On the other side of the room, Beth was still snoring away, none the wiser to what Sarah had just been through.

Over the next hour, light from the outside slowly began to creep through the window and brighten up the dark recesses of the bedroom with a haze, deep amber.

Sarah stared up at the ceiling once more. Hoping to any and all gods that she could get a single hour of dreamless sleep before everyone else would wake.

*

As the pale yellow sun climbed higher into the morning sky, it retreated behind a set of pendulous, heavy clouds. The leaden grey sky, though rainless, hid the day and cast a bleakness over the Appalachians. Everything was silent. The day's wildlife was still in hiding as the night creatures began their retreat.

Breaking this silence, heavy footsteps echoed through the trees surrounding the northern point of Chattooga National Park. For the past forty minutes, Juno had been out running, like she did most mornings. Sweating out the alcohol from the previous night.

Though only wearing Lycra leggings and a sports halter top, she did not feel the chilly remnants of the night air, only the pounding of her feet on the ground and the warming sweat that dripped down her back. The silver pendant around her neck flailed to and fro with each step.

That day, Juno pushed herself more than she had done in a while. Just when she would normally slow down to regain some strength, she exerted herself even harder. She had to. She didn't deserve anything less than to feel every muscle pang she could force. She believed she deserved this punishment. After everything that had happened over the past year, she deserved at least this.

Seeing Sarah again had sent her on a silent spiral she needed to mask. The guilt and pain had flooded back as soon as she arrived at the cabin. And because of this, the pendant around her neck that brought her so much joy felt so much heavier. But she could never take it off, despite what it brought with it.

Once her feet left the dirt-and-leaf floor and hit the gravel of the cabin's car park, Juno finally slowed her pace. And as she did, her legs throbbed with a warming soreness. Through gritted teeth, she took in a large lungful of air to steady her breath and tucked the pendant back into her top.

In her room, Rebecca sat on the edge of her bed, still dressed in her pyjamas. Wearing sunglasses, she ran her hand through her mass of messed-up hair resembling a large bushel of branches. She pulled her fingers through the knots accumulated during the night.

Her head spun as her stomach turned, feeling the intense after-effects of the wine she knew she should have not drunk.

She had sat motionless for a few minutes, hoping the effects would dissipate. But when they remained, she knew she was in this for the long haul.

Before she could lie back to try to grab more sleep, footsteps in the hallway caught her attention. The door opened wide.

"Wakey, wakey," Juno hollered as she strode in.

Rebecca slowly tilted her head up to Juno's grinning, wide-awake face. She audibly grimaced and slumped her head into her hands.

"Not feelin' too good?" Juno asked, closing the door. "Better get ready. We got caves to do."

"I feel like goddamn roadkill." Rebecca sighed again as she stood up from the bed. "Give me five minutes, okay?

Maybe ten." She walked into the bathroom and, before she closed the door, glanced back at Juno. "Maybe thirty."

The bathrooms in the cabin were wood-panelled and quite basic. They felt too small, especially for someone of Rebecca's height. She ducked under the beam running the width of the room and undressed, hitting her arms and legs on the walls.

Reaching out, she grabbed the shower's tap and stared up at the slightly rusted showerhead. She closed her eyes, preparing herself for what she was about to do, what she had to do to shock her out of this hangover.

In her bathroom, Beth stared at herself in the mirror above the sink. Looking regretfully at her bloodshot eyes, she stuck out her tongue and studied its blotchy white texture.

"Just had to have one more drink, didn't you?" she grumbled.

Suddenly, a scream rang out from Rebecca's bathroom that ripped Beth away from her self-disgust.

But Beth chuckled. She had been on holiday with Rebecca before. She had drunk all night with Rebecca before, when Rebecca had screamed the following morning during her cold shower. Sure, the first time it happened, Beth had rushed into Rebecca's bathroom, where she had expected to find a crazed intruder murdering Rebecca. Instead, she found her naked and hungover in the shower, cursing at the cold water.

Sam walked into the kitchen, as hungover as the rest, but before she could even register what was happening she was met by a smiling Juno, who stood by the counter with one leg on top of it, stretching out her calves.

"Good morning," Juno said loudly, relishing the fact that everyone felt worse than she did. She lunged forward in her stretch.

"Good? Is that what you call it?" Sam mumbled in reply.

From the hallway, Holly emerged. "It's too early for all this noise." She made a beeline for the kettle.

"We'll be leaving at seven o'clock sharp," Juno added as she moved her leg off the counter and headed for her bedroom. "Don't be late, guys."

"She's far too happy," Holly said under her breath, flicking the kettle on. "Big show-off."

Sam slumped onto a kitchen chair and groaned a wordless response.

"We probably shouldn't have had the whisky," Holly said as she wiped the cold sweat from her forehead.

"Can I get a coffee?" Sam asked almost pitifully.

With a nod, Holly then kicked one leg up onto the kitchen counter, mimicking Juno's stretching. "I declare that the queen is dead," she said, turning to Sam as she lunged more lithely and a lot farther than Juno could. "Long live the new fucking queen."

Walking out of the bathroom, Rebecca was dressed in her sports bra and pants while she dried her hair with a towel.

Juno sat by her bed, picking up gear from the pile at the foot of it and packing it into her bag.

Without saying a word, Rebecca slung the towel over

her shoulder and walked over to the dresser. Grabbing a small crucifix on a chain from the top, she undid the clasp and attached it around her neck.

In Sarah and Beth's room, Beth was still in the bathroom and Sarah sat on the edge of her bed, knocking back some pills she had swallowed dry. Her face was drawn and tired after her restless night.

Sarah hung her head and closed her eyes. "Love each day," she whispered like a mantra. "You can do this. You just gotta get through one day." She took a breath and closed her eyes even tighter. "Love each day."

"Alright, girls! Group shot," Holly shouted as she adjusted the tilt on the camera resting on the Jeep's hood.

Dressed in a tight-fitting winter coat, with her hair expertly messy, Holly's hangover from an hour prior was a thing of the past, just like it was for Juno.

The rest of the group all stood on the cabin's veranda. They each looked slightly fragile, and their hangovers still lingered.

"Okay, give us a smile, you miserable bastards!" Holly commanded, and she pressed the timer button on the camera and ran over to get in shot.

"I look and feel like boiled arseholes," Beth said morosely.

"You all look like one, too." Holly beamed. "Now, smile!"

Within a split second, all six of them suddenly mugged for the camera—each temporarily forgetting any ill feeling. For the first time since they'd arrived at the cabin, they looked like a single group. A group having an amazing time.

*

The Chattooga National Park was vast and one of the largest on the eastern seaboard. But unlike other national parks, this one only had vague boundaries. This far out into the wild of the Appalachians, with all the animal habitats to protect and the rugged terrain stretching across the ranges, the park's limits were more conceptual than physical. The dense forests, winding rivers, and cliffs made it nearly impossible to draw definitive lines.

It wasn't just the sheer size of the park that contributed to this border ambiguity, but also natural barriers that had shifted over time. Erosion, landslides, and seasonal changes altered the landscape, making it hard to map precisely. In some places, the park blended seamlessly with the surrounding wilderness, creating an impression that it had no true end and rolled over the mountains and valleys. For the park, there was only one entrance sign from the single track, with no fences or exit signs. The only way you could know for sure if you left the park was when you hit the city limits of a neighbouring town.

Seven kilometres north of the cabins at the entrance to the park, up the steep track on a seemingly never-ending forest road, two four-by-four vehicles navigated along its uneven path. The sprawling canopy of trees stretched thickly over them, blocking out any meagre sunlight that managed to find its way through the overcast sky.

Ahead, in the first and larger vehicle, Juno drove, with Sarah beside her in the passenger seat. Beth sat in the back on her own. The bumpy journey rocked them all about and the vehicle's poor suspension did little to help.

Sarah paid this uneven terrain no mind as she, once again, found herself staring out of the window. Her gaze was just as distant and unfocused as it always seemed to be lately. The view was moving too fast and frantically to stare at anything in particular, so her eyes just glossed over the blurry haze.

Then, from the corner of her eye, deep in a shadowy part of the forest, a streak of yellow light caught her attention. Yet, when she turned her gaze to focus on it, it vanished. Squeezing the bridge of her nose between her thumb and forefinger, she closed her eyes tightly for a second.

"Everything alright?" Beth called out to her from the back seat.

Juno turned to Sarah with a worried look. "You okay, doll? Need me to stop?"

"No, no, I'm good," Sarah lied, shaking her head. "Just the wine coming back to slap me in the face."

"We can still turn back, Sarah... if you want," Beth added, much to the chagrin of Juno, who shot her a stern glance in the rear-view mirror.

Juno, not wanting to have anything dampen this excursion, butted in. "You'll love it. It'll be just what you need. I planned it all perfectly with you in mind!"

Beth stared at the back of Juno's head, her frustration equal to her subdued anger. She wanted to shout at Juno for being selfish, for making everything about her once again, and for not realising that Sarah may not have been ready for this much so soon. But she knew that if she said a thing, an argument would break out, and that would be just as bad for Sarah.

Though this didn't stop Beth from imagining her screaming at Juno, and as she pictured the tirade she wanted to aim at her, the guilt of convincing Sarah to come weighed heavier than ever on her shoulders.

In the vehicle behind them, Rebecca was driving, with Sam in the passenger seat. Between them was Holly, leaning in from the back seat, a camcorder firmly in her grip as she filmed their journey.

Rebecca glanced at her sister, who was busy fiddling with her plastic watch, a plastic water bottle held between her legs. "You should drink some of that." She nodded to the bottle.

Sam didn't look up and continued fiddling with her watch. "You know you don't have to tell me that every single second of the day, right?"

"What are you doing with that watch?" Holly asked.

"The buttons are too bloody small," Sam sighed. "It's impossible to set the bloody time on this thing!"

"Bin it, then," Holly replied as she aimed her camera's viewfinder at her.

"It was the first thing Josh ever gave me." Sam jabbed at the button on the watch repeatedly, to no effect. "He set the alarm to go off every day at three. That's when he finished his shift. That's how I knew he'd be coming home."

"Josh." Holly chuckled. "Your kind-of, sort-of boyfriend?"

"That's the one." Rebecca smiled.

Sam paid them no attention.

Holly laughed. "That's mental. If any fella gave that thing to me, I'd dump him on the spot!"

Sam stopped playing with her watch. "So, you done Boreham Caverns before, Becca?"

"You asked me that, too. You worried about it?" Holly asked.

"Nothing to be concerned about. They're just level two, quite safe and simple," Rebecca said. "You've done harder in the climbing centre."

"Why do you both think I'm worried?" Sam protested. "I'm fine."

"Well, even so, there's no danger, according to the guidebook," Rebecca added.

Holly turned her camera to Rebecca. "I think the only real danger is that I might fall asleep while in there. I guarantee it'll be for kids. Probably should be renamed Boredom Caverns, not Boreham."

Rebecca glossed over Holly's comment and motioned to the water bottle held between Sam's legs. "Now, drink up. You want me to stop bugging you about it? Have some. It's a big-sister commandment."

With a huff, Sam grabbed her water bottle, flicked the lid open, and gulped.

"There's a track up on the left here," Sarah said, mostly certain. "Is that the one you want?"

Juno scanned the road, seeing where Sarah pointed. Suddenly, her eyes lit up. "Aw, hell yeah! Let's go off road!"

In the back seat, Beth looked ill, feeling like she might throw up from the hangover and the subsequent tumultuous drive. "Off road?" she said sarcastically. "Oh, yes. That's just what I need right now."

The four-by-four quickly swerved left, off the main track and onto a smaller dirt one, heading deeper into the thickening wilderness. Dust kicked up a cloud behind them as the wheels spun.

A few feet behind them, Rebecca followed in their vehicle and matched the pace as best she could.

Juno gripped the steering wheel and looked gleeful as she raced the four-by-four up the small track.

Beside her, Sarah looked very uneasy at the speed they were going, but she kept her thoughts to herself as she gripped the door handle tightly.

"Are you sure this is the right way?" Beth shouted over the roaring engine.

"You been here before, Beth?" Juno retorted. "No, I didn't think so. Now, relax, I've never been lost in my life." She whooped again with an almost offensive air of self-belief.

The vehicles charged around another bend on the mountain track, throwing up large plumes of dust and dirt in their wake. Neither one of them was relenting, both hurtling along.

Higher and higher and farther and farther away from the cabin they went.

Another patch of rough terrain threw them about in their respective vehicles until Juno slammed on the brakes and forced the four-by-four to an abrupt halt.

Rebecca bore down close behind but veered around them, skidding in the soft mud as she hit on the brakes. Her bumper ended up a few inches farther than Juno's. In this ruleless game, Rebecca felt she won. Juno got there faster, but she got farther.

"Nice parking," Holly said from the back seat, still filming everything.

"Why, thank you, young lady," Rebecca replied as she unclipped her seat belt.

"I take it we're walking from here?" Sam asked, jabbing at her watch's buttons.

"No idea." Rebecca shrugged. "That's a Juno question. I've got no idea where we are."

"I didn't see any signs on the way either," Holly added. "You sure she hasn't lured us out into the woods to kill us?"

Sarah climbed out of the passenger seat, closely followed by Beth. She walked around the back to get their equipment.

Juno, meanwhile, was still in the driver's seat. She removed the keys out of the ignition and hid them up behind the sun visor, out of sight. Not that anyone out this far in the Appalachians would be looking to steal a hired car.

Then, checking on Sarah and Beth in the mirrors, Juno quietly pulled the small, dog-eared copy of Caving in Chattooga from her pocket and tucked it into the glove compartment. She peered around with a satisfied smile.

The group stood around in a circle. The woods around them were thick and shadowed. The sky above, a deeper darker grey than before. Each dressed in climbing gear, complete with helmets, gloves, ropes strapped over their shoulders, and all manner of tools hanging off belts. Each of them also had a compact rucksack strapped onto their backs.

"Let's get moving," Juno said excitedly. "We're running late."

"How far is it from here?" Beth asked.

"Not that far," Rebecca answered before turning to Juno. "Right?"

Juno smiled enigmatically before turning to walk farther upward.

Sarah looked at Beth. "Where's your whistle?"

With a smile, Beth pulled out an old train conductor's whistle from her shirt pocket, brandishing it with a flourish. Popping it in her mouth, she blew a couple of loud toots.

"Why do you have that?" Holly asked.

"It's my good luck charm," Beth replied. "As long as I have it, I have the luck, too!"

As they all began their trek, Beth called out, "Hey, Juno, you do know where we're going, don't you?"

"There's a river about half a mile ahead," Juno answered tersely without slowing her pace. "When we reach it, we need to follow it north to the mouth of the cave."

Sam, at the back, tapped Rebecca on the shoulder. "How does she know there's a river ahead?"

"She can probably smell it," Holly deadpanned.

Rebecca shook her head. "She came up here last week to check the route out. Rule number one of hers, know the flight plan and stick to it."

"What's rule number two, then?" Sam added.

"Don't go wandering off," Rebecca said as they ascended a steeper incline. "You think it's dark when the lights are out? Down there, it's nothing like you've ever seen before."

After a ten-minute hike farther up, the group arrived at a flat elevation. Nearby, flowing water trickled between boulders.

"Told you." Juno smirked at Beth.

In front of them, white water sloshed down a narrow gully, leading back down the rock.

Rebecca, meanwhile, was still lecturing Holly and Sam at the back of the group. "You can get dehydration, disorientation, claustrophobia—"

Sam glanced at Holly and rolled her eyes in boredom.

"—panic attacks, paranoia, and hallucinations, visual and aural."

Juno, a dozen paces in front of everyone else, led them all up a ridge beside the river.

As they reached the top, a group of large crows scattered upward into the air in a frantic flurry. Once they'd walked farther along the ridge, they saw where the crows had been: the rotten corpse of a giant elk. Its huge bulk was deflated and gaunt, its fur matted with blood and mud, its body littered with pecking holes.

As the group gathered around the animal, Rebecca and Sam studied it, while Sarah and Beth turned away in disgust.

Holly, meanwhile, filmed the animal's corpse with her camcorder.

"Cool," she mumbled.

"Lovely," Beth said with a grimace. "A real Kodak moment."

Wishing to take a closer look, Sam got down on her haunches.

"Hey, don't touch it," Rebecca cut in.

"Yeah, don't touch it. You don't wanna piss it off," Beth countered.

"Just looking at it a bit closer, that's all," Sam said.

Sarah glanced back as Sam examined its neck wound. "What do you think did that, Sam? A bear or something?"

"Or a cougar," Holly added, still filming the animal.

Sam shrugged. "Actually, I think it was just sick. No wounds except the bird marks."

Exasperated, Juno threw her arms in the air. "What is this, frickin' Nature Detectives or something? It could have been Bigfoot for all you know—or a chupacabra."

Not needing any clairvoyance to sense Juno's frustration, Rebecca clapped her hands together. "Come on, now. Let's go! Let's leave this big guy in peace."

Continuing up to the next plateau, they approached a small waterfall with an easily climbable incline on one side.

Seeing it, Juno's face lit up. "Just up here and to the left." She hurried her pace. "This is it!" Juno called out once she reached the top of the small waterfall, not waiting for the rest of her friends.

While she began to fight through the heavy foliage to the left, the others made it up to the level in a single file.

Beth and Sarah were first to arrive and follow Juno

through the foliage. When they did, they emerged into a clearing on the edge of a large sinkhole in the ground—a gaping black hole that went straight down.

"Oh, you are having a fucking laugh," Beth exclaimed as she stared into the pit.

"'Fraid not," Juno replied.

"For Christ's sake, Juno!" Beth spat. "I'm an English teacher, not bloody Tomb Raider."

Sam peered back over her shoulder through the foliage and, for the first time, realised how high up they truly were. Instead of looking into the sinkhole like all the others, she just stared at the view behind her. A view of the Chattooga National Park stretching out for an eternity. Forest-covered peaks as far as she could see.

Chapter 5

DEEP DOWN

From the thick blackness of the hole's depths, its cavernous entrance yawned to the grey skies overhead, vast and swallowing. The jagged tear in the ground let in the dim light that filtered down through the clouds, but it was quickly smothered by the shadows below. The walls leading down from the surface were slick with constant moisture, which glistened faintly like glitter in the dim daylight. Three ropes hung side by side, leading from off the edge, trailing deep down to the bottom of what, at first glance, looked like an impenetrable abyss.

Peering down into the sinkhole, all six women stood fully kitted up. Gone were their bulky raincoats, and they wore their figure-hugging climbing tops, leggings, and helmets affixed with headlamps.

Juno—wearing a custom cut-off wetsuit as her climbing outfit—had both hands on the rope, feet on the brim of the hole, as she leaned back over the nothing.

"I'll see you down there, losers," she said with a giggle.

With one hand, she reached up and switched on her

helmet's lamp. The light from it shone brightly into the dullness around her.

Grabbing the rope again, she let out a "Yeehaw!" as she pushed off the edge and expertly dropped.

She descended on her rope in a controlled fall, and the beam from her headlamp grew brighter and brighter the darker it became. The beam shot out in all directions as she glanced around. But there was nothing to be seen except uneven, rocky walls. Having previously tested the depth of the hole with a falling rock, Juno knew that she was about halfway down, and she loved every single second of it.

Glancing up, she caught sight of Rebecca, Sam, Holly, Beth, and Sarah all looking down at her. But their view cut off as she fell deep below the veil of shadows that even her headlight could not outshine.

"So," Beth said, "we should just head back to the cabin and get fucked up on the rest of the wine, right?"

Everyone giggled except Sarah, who stared down into the hole, distracted.

"If I didn't think that I'd be murdered in my sleep for abandoning her, I would so be up for a round two of last night," Rebecca added.

Everyone knew this was a joke but also knew there was some degree of truth to it. No one wanted to get on the wrong side of Juno. No one had the commitment to do that.

Holly kept her camera firmly pointed down, but on her viewfinder, only blackness could be picked up by the lens.

Finally hitting the bottom, Juno planted her feet

firmly on the smooth rock beneath her. Unhooking her harness from the rope, she peered around the cavern. With childlike glee, she marvelled as her headlamp illuminated the shimmering stalagmites littering the edges of the cave floor. Juno mused that the stalagmites looked like an alien welcoming party, standing in wait as they entered their strange world.

"You dead down there?" Holly screamed from high above, her voice reverberating down through the shadows.

"You've got to see this place," Juno shouted back as she scanned the cavern, awestruck, looking at every part of the rock formations. "It's so beautiful."

Her voice echoed and resonated around her.

Taking a big breath in, she couldn't hold back her joy. She was truly in her element.

Rebecca pulled on Sarah's harness wrapped around her waist and thighs. "Looking good," she said as she turned to Beth.

With only one leg in her harness, Beth looked at it, confused. "Where the hell do I put my other leg?" she moaned, peering up to Rebecca. "Little help for this old lady, huh?"

Shaking her head with a chuckle, Rebecca stepped over and helped Beth with her straps.

"So, we're really doing this, are we?" Sarah asked, half joking.

"You'll love it." Rebecca didn't turn around, finishing securing Beth's harness around her waist. "Remember '97? The bungee jump? You didn't believe us until we forced you into it." Then she turned to address the others. "And everyone, remember to check your equipment. You should have five cams. These are the little things you can shove in a crack in the rock to hold ropes and things." She motioned to the collection of thin spring-loaded camming devices hanging from her belt. "Also, in your bags, you should have some snap lights, and you have a couple small grappling devices called grapnels, which can hold much more weight than a cam. Juno has the first aid kit, and I have the food. Any questions... just ask me or Juno, okay?"

"Becca, darling," Holly chirped up as she shut the viewfinder of her camcorder, then fixed it to a mount on the side of her helmet. "You said in the car that these caves were level two or rated two or something?"

Rebecca turned to her. "Yeah, I did. What about it?"

"Forgive such a newbie question, but what, pray tell, does that mean?" Holly smiled. "Is that a good thing? I mean, for all I know, level two may mean full of snakes."

"You don't know?" Sam piped in.

"My sport's above ground normally, up buildings," Holly replied. "And we grade it as high, very high, and very fucking high."

"Most caves are now rated by number," Rebecca explained as she picked up two harnesses from her pack and then handed them to Holly and Sam. "One is easy. Got guide ropes, all flat surfaces. For kids. Two is moderate for adult beginners. Just a fun cave with some nice inclines and walls to scale."

"What does it go up to?" Holly asked.

"Top is five. Loads of tough sections, waterlogged caverns. Basically, don't go unless you know what the hell you are doing, and even then, you shouldn't try it. And above that, there's no more grading, 'cause it's ungraded and not for humans to try if they wanna live."

"You ever done a five?" Sarah said.

Rebecca shrugged. "Sure. But I really don't like them. They don't feel like fun at all. They're like gauntlets that can kill you. Juno, though, keeps wanting to drag me to them. I swear she gets a lady boner every time she finds a level five."

"A what now?" Holly laughed.

After all their straps and harnesses were secure, side by side, Beth and Sarah descended on their ropes into the sinkhole. Their headlamps on, their gloved hands gripping the thin polyamide that held their weight.

Beth's eyes were wide, obviously not enjoying the ride. "Oh shit, oh shit, oh shit," she muttered as she did her best not to panic.

Sarah was the first of them to smoothly reach the bottom, met by a grinning Juno. Beth, though, was still a good fifteen feet up, her descent more stuttered and off-kilter.

Like Juno had done, Sarah looked around at all the rocks that may as well have been from a different planet. "Wow."

Juno smiled. "Told you, didn't I?"

Beth, finally reaching the bottom, was already out of breath.

"You need a nap now, Beth," Juno quipped.

Beth didn't rise to the jibe and just let go of her rope. She stared around the cave next to Sarah and said in awe, "Oh my god."

Juno felt a swell of pride. She knew she had picked the right place, knew she was right in deciding this whole trip. Then again, she always thought she was right. But it was good to get affirmation.

"I had no idea it would be like this," Sarah said as her headlamp brought light to things that may never have been lit before.

"It's quite something," Beth added as she turned to Juno with a sincere expression. "It's incredible, Juno."

Before Juno could reply, a loud "Wooo!" sounded from high above.

Holly, unlike the others, was not inclined to take this slow. She may not have gone caving before, but she knew ropes and harnesses all too well. Travelling at great speed into the darkness, she hollered all the way down, the camcorder affixed to her helmet.

"Jesus," Beth exclaimed as she stared at the almost-free-falling Holly.

Before any real panic could set in, and at the last possible moment, Holly slowed her fall and landed on the rock like a cat with a large grin.

Sarah smiled, finding Holly endearing and hilarious. Beth had no idea what to feel, having just felt like she nearly witnessed a death. Juno, though, was not happy.

"Holly, this isn't some damn MTV-bungee-jump

bullshit," she chided. "We do this safely. In order. Following my lead. You get me?"

"Is it clear down there?" Rebecca called from above.

"Yeah, all clear," Sarah shouted and stepped back from the centre of the rock, guiding Beth back with her hand to break the tension.

Up top, Rebecca fussed over Sam's harness, triple-checking it.

"I have done this before, you know," Sam complained.

"Not with me, you haven't," Rebecca replied as she checked the harness. "I'm only looking out for my sister."

"And I appreciate that but only in small doses."

Quickly getting the hint, Rebecca stood back and nodded. "Fair enough. I'll try to remember."

Rebecca always wanted to be a real big sister to Sam but felt that Sam pushed back, resenting her for some reason. It was not her fault their father played the field, that Sam was a child of an extramarital affair. But she was happy Sam was even here.

After checking her own harness, she grabbed a rope and Sam followed suit.

"Race ya," Sam said with a cheeky grin.

On the way down, Sam sped up, wanting a small victory in this, her half-sister's domain. But as she neared the final ten feet, Rebecca whizzed past and landed expertly, managing to unhook herself before Sam's feet even touched down.

Once she landed, Sam took in the beauty of the cave around them as their headlamps illuminated the rocks brightly—all except Holly, who was filming the group.

A few feet away, Juno stood beneath a steady stream of water descending from the mouth of the cave, which soaked her brow.

"Juno?" Sam asked, a tinge of worry in her voice. "That story you told us of the flooded cave..."

"What about it?" Juno turned to listen.

"Well"—Sam gulped—"there's a river just up there and water coming in. Do you think there's any danger of—"

"You told her about Haverlock Caverns, didn't you?" Rebecca almost shouted at Juno.

"Yeah, so what?" Juno replied dismissively, wiping the water from her brow.

Rebecca turned to Sam. "Don't listen to her. And, no, this cave system is not known to flood. We checked it. Ever since they opened the caves a few decades ago, there's been zero instances of even a small flooding."

"What's Haverlock Caverns?" Beth asked.

Holly walked between Beth and Rebecca, aiming her camera at the nearly fifteen-foot stalagmite in front of her. "Men go in cave, water comes in, men get squished into rocks. The end."

"What the hell?" Beth exclaimed.

Rebecca glanced at Juno again. "You do this every time."

Juno smiled with a shrug.

Rebecca shook her head. "It's just a scary story that has nothing to do with this, okay?" She turned to Sam. "Juno's just trying to freak you out."

"Well, it worked," Sam replied.

Beth rolled her eyes to Sarah.

Nothing had to be said, as Sarah knew full well what that meant, that this was another thing Beth would hold against Juno.

The air around them, though cold, was tinged with a smell that tingled in their throats. A slight tang of ammonia, mixed with an earthy, mouldy musk. The moisture on the walls released a sour, metallic odour the closer you got to them—like rusted iron mixed with dead leaves.

Turning, Sarah disconnected herself from the conversation and studied the rock towering above her. As she shone her headlamp upon it, it highlighted long, thin scratch marks at eye level. Peering high above, then back down to the rock, she could only assume some poor animal got trapped down here and tried to claw its way out. Around the immediate floor, she saw no remnants of any creatures, so she presumed they must have gotten out—or gone in farther. Her attention was then drawn to a dark crevice in the cave wall ahead. It stood a few feet tall, and from within she thought she could hear a quiet chirping. She took a step closer.

"Sarah?" Juno called out.

But Sarah was too distracted. She moved carefully towards the crevice, towards the chirping.

"Guys," she whispered. "I think I've found a bird's nest in the wall."

Everyone quickly turned their attention to her as she unclipped a flashlight from her belt, switched it on, then aimed the beam into the crevice's shadows.

"Sarah, step back," Juno said with urgency. "They're not bir—"

The crevice erupted with a multitude of small flapping shapes. Black and frantic blurs billowed out in a swarm towards Sarah.

Bats.

Many bats.

With a panicked scream, Sarah was frozen, lacking the reflexes to jump out of this line of fire. But Juno's hand quickly shot out, grabbed her by the shoulder, and yanked her backwards. Clearing her out of the way of the swarm fluttering chaotically up towards the mouth of the sinkhole.

Juno, appearing unaffected, released her shoulder. "It's okay. They're not going to hurt you."

"Are you sure?" Sarah replied.

"Take a look for yourself." Juno pointed up to the bats swirling about the funnel of the entrance in an elegant spiral.

Everyone looked at them with a smile. After their shocking entrance, seeing these bats circling high above was an eerie yet beautiful sight.

Holly turned her camcorder up to film. "Like butterflies of the night," she said softly.

"Oh, fuck off, Holly," Beth guffawed.

Sarah nodded to Juno silently in thanks.

"How did you know they weren't birds?" Sam asked.

"Aside from that, birds would not nest underground," Juno replied as she scrunched up her nose. "You can kind of smell the guano."

"Right, guys," Beth said loudly. "Now that the butterflies of the night have left the belfry, which way do we go?"

"Only one way in and one way out." Juno stepped up, pointing to the far side of the cavern entrance. "Follow that water down that pipe."

The water that dripped down the walls of the entrance gathered and flowed to the lowest point, where Juno pointed with glee to a crack in the cavern floor, only two feet wide and devoid of any light.

In the narrow, vertical shaft leading from the entrance chamber, Juno led the group down. With an abundance of footholds and rocks to grasp, this "pipe" was something even the most inexperienced caver could manage.

Even Beth, who was fourth in line, found this climb remarkably easy, so much so that the dread feeling in the pit of her stomach quelled. She was quite enjoying it.

"Remember, move feet and hands one at a time, guys," Juno called back. "Keep three parts held onto the rocks at once. Including you, Holly. No jumping around!"

The smell of bat waste faded, and what odour remained was more stagnant and much colder. A dense, empty mustiness.

One after the other, they climbed down the pipe, deeper into the mountain. Farther away from the daylight. At the end of the pipe, they found themselves in a long tunnel that levelled off to a shallow, downward slope.

Juno silently nodded in the direction they were to go.

"Watch your steps, guys," Rebecca said from the rear. "Even dry rock can be slippery. The last thing I want is for me to carry your fat asses back up top after you sprain an ankle."

As they slowly paced farther down the tunnel, each step brought them to a section that changed in size and shape. In one part, the walls seemed tall and thin, and in the next, the ceiling was quite low, the walls much wider.

One by one, they travelled in silence, occasionally stooping or turning to their side to pass through narrower rocks. The only sounds, aside from their breathing and echoed footsteps, were the collected moisture dripping from the ceiling above their heads.

Hearing Sam's louder-than-usual breaths, Sarah turned to her and whispered, "How are you feeling?"

"Exhausted." Sam smiled, keeping her voice low. "But don't tell Becca."

Rebecca, meanwhile, was at the back, oblivious. She was concentrating on watching everyone's feet, ensuring people stepped cautiously upon the rocks.

Farther and farther they travelled in single file through tunnel after tunnel, each of ever-changing sizes. Juno led their way confidently, so much so that the group felt little in the way of trepidation, like they were being led by someone who knew what they were doing. Who knew where they were going.

Even Beth, who harboured plenty of unspoken resentment towards Juno, was glad she was leading. Despite everything, Juno was undeniably the most experienced caver she had met, and Beth wouldn't feel as safe with anyone else down here. She didn't have to be her best friend to think that.

Soon, they came to a tunnel with a large crack in the wall at one end, a thin fissure only a foot wide and a few feet tall.

"Hold up, guys," Juno said.

Everyone halted in their tracks.

"Now is as good a time as any," she said as she turned to face the queue behind her.

Their headlamps and torches filled the small passage they were in, illuminating Juno. Her darker complexion was ghostly pale in the white light.

"Rebecca, you ready back there?" Juno called out, reaching up and switching off her headlamp.

"Sure thing," Rebecca replied, also turning off her headlamp and torch.

Holly turned, and her headlight caught Rebecca's smiling face.

"This is to show you all something that few ever really experience," Juno said. "And it's one of my favourite things to do." After a dramatic pause, she continued. "Turn all your lights off. Every single one of them."

"What?" Beth exclaimed. "I—"

"Just do it, Beth."

Sarah, Sam, and Holly turned their headlamps and torches off. Holly even powered down her camera. Its LED power light quickly flickering off.

Beth was last. But before she switched her lights off, she stared at Juno. "I want you to know this is bullshit."

As Beth flicked her headlight off, the darkness in the

tunnel appeared in full force. It wasn't just an absence of light but a suffocating absence of hope. Despite having no weight or bearing to it, this pitch black enveloped the group like a solid presence.

The closeness of the uneven walls melted away. Within this dark, it felt like there was nothing around them, as if the very darkness itself had turned the tunnel into an infinite void.

"Well, this is just a shit feeling, innit?" Holly chuckled, though her tone showed her nervousness. "It's like being buried."

"Jesus, I'm sweating," Beth added.

"Just feel the dark," Juno said.

This feeling pressed in on Beth more than anyone else—thick and oppressive, like being crushed. It felt so strange, as if the floor might drop away at any moment. Her heartbeats quickened, as did her breath. She felt a wave of nausea. Without another passing heartbeat, she flicked on her headlight, bringing normalcy back to an unreal experience with a burst of light. Its beam shone directly on Juno's face, causing her to squint.

"Sorry, guys," Beth said, out of breath. "No can do."

"You okay?" Rebecca called out from the back.

"She's fine," Juno replied.

"I hated that, Juno," Beth said.

"Yeah," Juno mumbled. "We all know."

"So did I," Sam added.

Sarah smiled as she turned on her torch, and everyone else did the same. "I actually really liked it."

"Yeah?" Juno said, relieved.

"Yeah, it felt like sleep, like a deep sleep."

"More like a nightmare," Sam said.

"Or death," Beth retorted.

"So, once more unto the breach, dear friends," Juno said as she turned back to the small fissure in the wall.

After a few feet of squeezing through, they exited the small fissure into a much larger space. Juno took a few steps forward as she shone her headlamp around. When she realised that her light had disappeared into the blackness instead of hitting any walls, coupled with the deeper chill in the air, she couldn't hold back her delight.

"Ladies," she said aloud, her voice echoing around them, "I think we could all do with a bit more light." Grabbing a phosphorus flare from her belt, she removed the cap. Without a pause, she then struck the igniter with the abrasive sticker on the rear of the cap.

The flare hissed to life with a blinding, sudden intensity. Its harsh light fizzed as it devoured the darkness around them. The large cavern they stood in, once shrouded in an impenetrable black, leapt into sharp relief. Jagged and uneven, the eerie glow of the flare cast long, sinister shadows that danced and flickered.

These pillars of rock had been formed over millions of years, sediment built upward and downward over aeons. The flare in Juno's hand illuminated their real colours of yellow with sulphur and red with iron. Each rock glistened as if covered in a fine glitter.

The group stood awestruck at the sight.

"Fuck my arse!" Beth exclaimed, unable to find the adequate words to describe her awe. "Okay, Juno, this is great. This... is..."

As the flare crackled and spat, its sulphurous scent mixed with the cold, dead air of the cavern. The grandeur of where they stood gave each person the feeling of standing in a subterranean cathedral, almost Gothic in its grandiose design.

One by one, each stepped away from their formed line to look closer at their surroundings.

Juno, though, stayed in place, holding her flare aloft. "Feel free to look around," she said, despite the fact the group had already dispersed.

"But remember to watch your step at all times," Rebecca added urgently.

In this vast expanse, six individual pools of light moved around the dark, closer to the large rocks that sprouted out in all directions.

Sarah stood farther away from the rest as she held up one hand to a towering stalagmite. She ran her palm over its yellowed, rough texture and listened to the cavern's soundtrack of dripping water. A sound that resonated throughout the chamber. The others' voices were barely a murmur to Sarah as she focused her hearing on the rhythmical drip, drip, drip. She paused to take a deep breath in, feeling the cold air fill her lungs with a somewhat pleasant sting.

Then a noise.

She turned to her left and aimed her torch where she thought the sound had come from.

Nothing.

She waited, keeping still. Her torch remained aimed at a gap between two large boulders at the end of the chamber.

She swore she heard something, like a scraping of stone on stone.

With her curiosity taking hold, she took a cautious step closer to the boulders.

Then another.

Then another.

Slowly advancing, she stared, wide-eyed and alert. Her torch shone through the two rocks and exposed a hole between them. A gaping cleft beneath them and another rock resting across them. A natural doorway into a darkness beyond.

Behind her, the faint laughter seemed far, far away. She stared into the void. Her torch's light was unable to penetrate its thick shadow.

She listened intently, staring into the nothing. Waiting for an answer.

Nothing.

She waited more.

Still nothing.

Shaking her head, Sarah breathed a sigh of relief. She must have imagined the noise. Of course she did. What did she think would make it? More bats? Bigger bats?

A slam of boots on rock caused Sarah to reel in shock as Juno landed on top of the boulder next to her, perched on the edge, smiling with a mischievous grin.

"Find anything good?" Juno said.

"Jesus Christ!" Sarah replied in shock, laughing.

"You found Jesus? In there?"

Sarah sighed at the terrible joke.

"Anyway, sorry to pull you away from the cave-dwelling son of God," Juno said, leaping off the boulder and landing next to Sarah. "It's time to eat."

Chapter 6

THE FISSURE

Sitting on a large rock to one side of the cathedral-like cavern, five of the group ate from small packets of dried food Rebecca had handed out from her backpack. The phosphorus flare fizzed away on the rock beside them, spewing out its glowing fluorescence.

Holly, meanwhile, was busy taking photos with a small pocket camera. Its flash illuminated the cavern in quick, sharp bursts whenever she pressed the button.

A water bottle being passed around came to Juno, who took a small sip before calling out to Holly. "Hey, take a break. You need to eat!"

"Yeah," Holly replied as she kept taking pictures. "Just getting a few more shots. This place is way cooler than I thought it would be."

But Juno was barely listening, because she'd noticed Sarah staring off blankly into nothing. "You okay, babe?"

Shaking off the distraction, Sarah glanced at her and forced a thin smile. "Juno. I'm fine. I am not gonna break. Just enjoying the quiet."

"I know you are," Juno said as she edged closer. "I just wanted to say—there's nothing I can say." She took a slow breath. "And there is never a good time to say this, so I'll just say it now. I'm sorry I didn't stick around longer. After the... you know."

Sarah didn't reply.

"I'm bad with that stuff. And it was Paul. He..."

"And Jessica," Sarah added softly, her voice cracking as she said her daughter's name.

"L-Look, we—we're all here for you now, I just wanted to say. I didn't mean anything by leaving."

"No, no, it's all good," Sarah said as she stood. "I'm sorry. I'm a bit out of it right now. Jetlag or hangover or something." Her words seemed forced. She just didn't want to think about all this. "I'm gonna have a look around, wake myself up a bit."

Juno nodded. "See if you can find the way through."

Sarah picked up her torch and walked off the rock.

"Don't go too far," Beth called out.

Holly had listened to Juno and Sarah's exchange. Leaning forward, she asked, "Hey, Juno, she alright?"

"She's fine," Juno replied, deadpanning.

"After the crash, she broke down pretty badly," Beth explained, keeping the same low volume. "Spent ages in hospital. She was a mess. Couldn't find a reason to get up in the mornings. I looked after her as much as I could."

"Well, I guess she found a reason to get up now, if she's here."

For a while, no one talked. They just finished their

packets of dried food and passed around the water bottle one more time.

Sam was sitting on the edge of the rock, shining her torch across a wall across from her, studying its jagged, uneven surface. She swore she saw it move. Or saw something move on it.

"Are there any animals down here?" she asked.

"Aside from you?" Holly chuckled.

"Could be, sure," Rebecca answered. "Animals get stuck in caves all the time. But few would survive the fall. I haven't seen any carcasses, though, so who knows? How come?"

"Hmmm." Sam looked away from the wall. "Nothing, just seeing things, I guess."

"Shadows do that to you," Rebecca added. "Make you see all kinds of stuff. So, if you see anything, it's probably not real. Just your mind trying to make sense of the dark."

"I think I've found the way to go," Sarah said, appearing suddenly at Juno's shoulder and startling her.

At the far end of the chamber from where they had entered, the walls converged to meet at the base of a small heap of scree and sediment. At the top of the pile, a narrow fissure led deeper down.

Rebecca and Juno stood in front of it, shining their lights inside.

"I don't understand," Rebecca said in confusion, staring into the fissure. "It's not how I imagined it from reading that book. All passages should be open and easy. The last one and this one... They are level three, at least."

Juno shrugged. "That's the trouble with these books. It's all about interpretation. What's easy to some isn't for others."

"Or I read it wrong," Rebecca added.

"No, you didn't." Juno smiled. "But it's only a tight squeeze through and then..."

"Then?"

"Then it should open out into a wider passage, like they always do!"

"If you say so." Rebecca sighed. "It's your party."

"Something wrong?" Sarah asked, walking over after overhearing the last part of their conversation.

Rebecca shook her head. "It's nothing. Where's Sam?"

"No idea. She was behind me a minute ago." Turning, she called out, "Sam, where are you?"

No response.

Everyone waited silently.

While they did, Sarah heard something faintly. Something she had heard before. Something she knew was not there. A giggle. A high-pitched, childlike giggle.

Ignoring it, she called out again, "Sam?"

"Dammit." Rebecca exhaled. "I told everyone to keep close at all times." Storming off into the cave, she shouted "Sam!" a few more times. Each time sounded more annoyed than the last.

Then, a voice called out from behind a rock to the left. A very annoyed voice. "I'm bloody busy. Can't you just shut up and wait!" Sam yelled. "And don't come back here."

"Hope it's not a number two!" Holly burst out laughing.

"Bugger off! I'm not having a shit in a cave!"

Rebecca shook her head. "This one's on me. I made her drink loads of water this morning."

"You guys can go on," Sarah said. "I'll wait for her here."

Holly, with a candy bar in hand, had already wormed her way in front of Juno and stood first in line at the fissure they all needed to traverse.

"I'll take point, yeah?" she asked confidently before she took a big bite of the bar.

Juno hooked a rope onto Holly's belt, then motioned with a sweeping hand for her to step into the fissure.

"Aw, yeah." Dropping her half-eaten candy bar to the floor, she moved into the fissure without a single moment's hesitation. She clipped her torch and small camera to her belt, then pressed record on the camcorder affixed to her helmet. "Let's do this!" She stooped down and squeezed herself through the narrow opening.

Within a couple of minutes, Holly was farther and deeper into the fissure than she'd imagined it would go.

Around her, rocks had started to funnel inward from her very first step. With each step, Holly had to turn her body, crouch, and twist to get around the ever-changing shape. She did not have a problem at first, not until the rocks began pressing down on her, eventually forcing her to lie flat and crawl over its uneven surface.

"It's a bit tight in here," she called back, downplaying the cramped rocks.

At the entrance, Beth shone her torch into the narrow crawlspace. Her face detailed her apprehension.

"You'll be in and through quick enough," Juno assured, patting Beth on the back.

Headfirst, Holly pulled herself through the intensely claustrophobic passage. The rocks around her dipped and rose. One moment she could turn her head, and the next she had to twist at a ninety-degree angle just to squeeze through. As her shoulder scratched against the edge of a jutting rock, she began to feel the fear.

Contorting herself through a sharp, awkward angle, Holly's breath quickened. Below her, a small pool of muddy water filled the stone basin, and to tilt her head to go through, she had put her face in the puddle.

It was then that she remembered the story Juno told them, and she could not help but imagine the rocks coming down and crushing her as water flooded the caves.

But just as the cold sweat broke out over her body, as her heartbeats began to race, she tilted her head into the water and pushed her body through, and then the small crawlspace grew wider and higher, allowing her to breathe a sigh of relief.

After a few more feet, Holly pulled herself out of the fissure, which opened into a large, open cavern. This one had tall, sloping walls, and the floor slanted as it stretched into the darkness.

The panic that had swelled through her stomach gave way to a rush of adrenaline. She punched the air.

Wiping her face clean of sweat and muddy water, Holly leaned back into the fissure, calling out to the others, "Okay, guys, I'm through it!"

"How far?" came Rebecca's faint reply.

"Uhh"—Holly shook her head—"between a hundred to a hundred and fifty feet, I guess?"

At the opposite side of the fissure, Juno, Rebecca, Sarah, Sam, and Beth waited.

"See?" Juno asked Rebecca with a satisfied smile. "Always leads to a bigger cave."

"Yeah," Rebecca answered, though still unsure. "I guess."

With a smirk, Juno walked over to the fissure, ducked under the low rock, and headed inside. "See ya on the flip side, homedawgs!" she called out as she disappeared.

Beth didn't want to but smiled at Juno's latest Americanism.

"Alright," Rebecca said, turning to her sister. "You're up next, then Sarah'll go behind you, then Beth, then me."

"Can I go last?" Sarah asked.

"Really? How come?"

"I think I'd feel better if I'm not in the middle of people."

"Okay, I'll go in your place. So, Sam, me, Beth, then you." She turned to the others. "You all good with that?"

As everyone nodded, Beth stepped beside Sarah and whispered, "We can still go back, if it's too much?"

"It's not the cave." Sarah shrugged. "I'm just not feeling it too much, but it'll be fine. I'll get through it. Then tonight. Wine. Lots of wine."

Beth stopped and put one hand on Sarah's shoulder. "Out of the two of us, I'm the coward. You're the brave one.

So, don't think for one second that you're gonna steal my crown by pretending to be scared." She leaned in and kissed Sarah on the cheek. "And, yes, tonight, I'll get so much wine down your throat that you can't stand up. Deal?"

"Deal!"

Along the fissure, the five remaining women scooted through the contracting, twisted space. Crawling slowly towards Holly, who waited on the other side.

Sarah crawled through the fissure behind the rest, and as she traversed the first few feet from the entrance, she could hear the phosphorus flare in the cavern behind her crackle and fizz away as the glowing light dimmed.

Right after she reached one section of the fissure where she could stand, Sarah was soon forced to crouch again and crawled into the next part.

Behind her, deep in the cavern, she heard something.

A thud.

No, she thought. It must be in my head. It's always in my head.

She carried on without even thinking about it.

Back in the cavern, within the dying flare's glow, a dark shadow reached down and picked up Holly's discarded candy bar from the rocky floor.

As the flare finally burnt out and the cavern was once again thrust into darkness, a vile growl followed by the rustling foil wrapper pierced the silence.

*

At the exit of the fissure, leading into the sloping tunnel, Holly and Juno helped Sam crawl out into the new area.

"If I didn't go back in the cave," Sam said, staggering to her feet, her face dripping with muddy water, "I definitely would have pissed myself in there."

"That bit where you gotta turn your head into the water, right?" Holly grinned as Sam nodded. "Brown-pants time all around."

"It was not scary." Juno shrugged.

"Fucking hell," Holly said, aghast. "What do you see as scary, then, crawling through a pit of leaky arseholes?"

In the dark fissure illuminated by her headlight, Rebecca crawled through, slowly and steadily. As she squeezed her head through the tightest part of the fissure, her head slicking through the dirty water, the ceiling opened higher for a few feet. As she moved, she did not notice the dust that fell from the cracks in the ceiling and floated down onto her helmet.

"Beth, you okay back there?" Rebecca called out behind her.

"Yeah," Beth said, sounding like she was not enjoying this. "Remind me why I agreed to this bullshit again?"

"You're coming up to a tight bit. Tilt to your left on the turn, okay? You may get a bit wet. But just tilt left, and it'll get a bit higher on the next bend."

Beth crawled forward and soon came upon the tight turn. Following Rebecca's advice, she twisted her body to the left and around the rock. And like Rebecca, she did not see the dust particles that fell from the ceiling.

"Sarah?" Beth called out as she turned. "You still alive?"

Ten feet behind, Sarah was breathing heavily.

"I think so," she replied.

She was having more difficulty than the others had. She never actually liked the thought of caving and had only agreed to this excursion because of Beth. It was all for Beth. For everything she had done over the past year. To thank her, but also to apologise for the times Sarah had screamed at her, aiming her grief unfairly. Also, Sarah knew that she needed to get out of her house. To get out of her own mind.

But she had not known until that moment that she almost definitely had some degree of claustrophobia.

The stone digging into her chest and the one scraping her back made her feel a terrifying sense of death.

You have to get through it, Sarah.

You have to get through it.

You have to get through it.

"Turn left when you get to the wet patch," Beth shouted. "Okay, that sounded all kinds of wrong."

"I'm okay," Sarah called back. "I'm coming."

Beth got the message. This wasn't quite the time for her jokes. So, she turned and carried on through the narrow fissure, hearing the other girls talking in the cavern ahead.

Shuffling along the best she could, Sarah approached the section where she had to twist to one side and submerge herself in the pool of stagnant water. But as she twisted her body to the left, as she tried to squeeze around the tight corner—something stuck her firmly in place, pinning her, with her cheek resting in the water.

She tried to move her shoulders but could not budge. She squirmed left and right but did not move. She was wedged in tight.

As Sarah tried to wriggle more, a plume of dust fell onto her from the ceiling above, hitting her in the face.

"Shit." She gasped as panic emerged. First, it was agitation, then annoyance, then pure fear. "Shit, shit, shit!"

Her breathing fell shallow and fast as the water splashed her face and into her mouth.

"Sarah," Beth called out. "What's happening?"

"I can't move!" Sarah shouted. "I'm stuck."

In the sloping cavern, Rebecca was helped out of the fissure by Holly.

On the far side of the space, Juno was busily exploring the rock formations while she waited for the rest to climb through.

"It's Sarah," Beth shouted to those in the cavern. "I think she might be stuck."

"There's no might be about it," Sarah yelled from behind. "Fuck! Fuck! FUCK!"

Beth turned her head. "Alright, Sarah. Try to calm down. Breathe slowly. You must relax."

"I can't fucking relax!" Sarah screamed in furious fear, sounding more frantic with each word. "I'm in the fucking dark, stuck in a fucking mountain, with my head in a fucking gross puddle."

"Sarah," Beth said calmly and evenly. "You have to listen to me, okay? You have to calm down. And the only way you can do that is to breathe slowly."

"I've got a million tonnes of rock above my fucking head, Beth," Sarah screamed, hyperventilating. "How the fuck am I supposed to calm down? I can't fucking breathe!"

She tried her best to twist her body, but the more she struggled, the more dust rained down on her from the ceiling.

Beth, reaching a wider part of the fissure, quickly turned herself around and then began crawling back to Sarah. She was so determined that she didn't even notice the rock scrape her side, grazing her skin through her thin top.

"Sarah, just listen to me," she said as she crawled hurriedly. "Listen to my voice."

In the sloping cavern, Holly leaned into the fissure entrance. "Everything okay in there, guys? Beth out yet?"

"I'm sure they'll be out in a sec," Rebecca said. "She can squeeze through. She's smaller than me."

"Don't worry," came Beth's echoey voice. "Just give us a minute."

In the darkness, with only the light of their headlamps, Beth and Sarah faced each other.

Within the span of a few minutes, Sarah had grown more and more desperate. More panicked. She had tried to turn her head, but as she did, more water got into her mouth. She spluttered and gagged, spitting the muddy grime out. The more she writhed against the rock, the more stuck she seemed to get.

"Please, get me out of here."

Every time Sarah tried to move, more dust fell from the rocks above. Beth, noticing it, sensed the danger that they could both be in.

"Look at me," Beth commanded, completely focusing on Sarah's eyes. "You calm down right now. Okay? Now, listen."

Sarah stopped her squirming, shocked into stillness by Beth's authoritarian tone.

"What are you most afraid of?"

"I can't move," Sarah said, agitated and terrified.

"You can. You can move." Beth's voice was calm yet firm. "It's just in your head. You think that because you can't move the way you think you should move, that you can't move at all. That's crap. If you can get in, you can get out. That's just physics."

"I can't stop panicking," Sarah whimpered.

"Sarah, listen to me. The worst thing that could happen to you... has already happened to you. The thing that you would fear the most."

Sarah, despite wanting to listen and do the sensible thing, was distracted by her panic.

"It's over," Beth continued. "And you're here right now on the other side of the world. You didn't give up then. And here and now? This is just a poxy little bloody cave. You've got nothing left to be afraid of. Especially from this stupid rock."

Hearing those words, Sarah calmed down, staring at her friend, as she realised how true they were. She had experienced far worse than this.

Outside of the fissure, Juno stood with the rest of them, also leaning in, listening to every word Beth and Sarah said. Though far inside, the sound travelled out to them on an echo.

"Sarah?" Beth said.

"Yeah?" Sarah replied weakly.

"You remember that slimy guy from college, Charlie Morgan? Head of the debating committee?"

At the exit, Juno cringed at the story, knowing what was about to be said.

Distracted momentarily from the dilemma and her panic, Sarah managed a small laugh. "Oh, him? How could I forget?"

"He was an asshole," Beth added.

"And so fucking arrogant, he could talk his way out of anything!"

"And into anything." Beth laughed. "Including Juno's bed!"

At the exit, Juno grimaced in embarrassment.

Holly, Sam, and Rebecca stood next to her, quiet as mice, also listening to every word.

"No!" Sarah said, wide-eyed. "You're kidding me! Those two?"

Beth could not help but smile. "Juno's had me sworn to secrecy for nearly ten years, on pain of death."

"I'm going to fucking kill you," Juno muttered.

Beth continued. "But after so long holding that secret in, and considering everything now, I figure some things are worth dying for!"

"I can't believe Juno fell for his bullshit."

"Next morning, neither could she." Beth's voice fell a lot quieter, so much so that the sound no longer travelled out of the tunnel. "And rumour had it, as Juno told me, he was not just a pain in the arse, but a real pain in the arse, if you know what I mean!"

The words may not have travelled to the rest of the group, but their subsequent laughter did.

Juno groaned, knowing what Beth had told Sarah.

Still laughing, Beth said, "Hey, I want you to crawl towards me, okay? But slowly this time. Nothing sudden."

With an unsure chuckle, Sarah nodded and shuffled back and forth, edging closer and closer towards Beth, feeling less stuck by the second.

"Slow. Take it slow." Beth backed down the fissure while Sarah approached her. "Okay, okay, that's good."

"I think I'm almost free," Sarah said with a small smile of relief, and she used her feet against the rock to push herself free.

But with that final effort, her boot accidentally kicked away rubble, causing the cave to snap and crack around them. As it did, the ceiling shifted and crumbled a couple of inches, stopping just above their helmets.

Both froze to the spot in horror, staring at each other. Their flashlights illuminated the other's face.

"Fuck," Beth whimpered. After a second's hesitation, she grabbed Sarah by the collar. "Move now!" she screamed as she heaved her backwards, pulling her free of the twisting turn.

Frantically, both scrambled backwards. When the fissure became a bit wider, Beth turned back around, and they scurried along the crawlspace.

Glancing over her shoulder, Sarah could only see the little that her headlamp illuminated.

But behind her rattled a horrible sound. A scuttling sound. Followed by a loud growl.

Beth did not hear a thing, too busy scrambling to get free, shouting, "Fuck, fuck, fuck, fuck, fuck, fuck!"

As the cave groaned with a loud crack, the fissure where Sarah had been stuck buckled, and the ceiling above it collapsed in on itself. Within the sound of the stone colliding, the terrifying shriek Sarah heard was quickly silenced.

But it was not over.

The whole structure had begun to cave in on itself, section by section, following them along the fissure as they raced.

Outside the fissure, Juno could sense exactly what was happening from the sound alone, but before she could throw herself into the narrow gap, Rebecca grabbed her arm and pulled her away.

"No!" Juno protested, trying to pull herself free.

"Juno, no!"

But Juno still pulled. "Sarah! Beth!"

(As she screamed, a cloud of thick dust erupted from the exit to the fissure, the collapse forcing the billow outward.

"Happy birthday!" Sarah said softly.

Her voice was filled with love as she placed the birthday cake in front of Jessica. The five candles flickered brightly in the dim living room, casting a soft glow on her daughter's innocent face.

Everything here felt perfect. The curtains had been drawn, the air warm, the scent of the freshly baked cake wafting through the air. A ballad played quietly from the kitchen radio behind them.

Jessica's wide eyes sparkled as she looked up at Sarah with a grin.

"Sarah?" she said—yet not in her voice.

It was Beth's.

"Sarah?" Beth shouted.

Juno's helmet lamp shone down on Sarah's dusty face as she slowly came back from unconsciousness.

When she opened her eyes, Rebecca held a bottle of water to her lips. "Sip it."

Before Sarah could gather her thoughts, a lungful of dirt caused her to cough and splutter.

In the dark, sloping area, with only their headlamps and torches to pierce the gloom, the dirt from the cave-in still hung heavily in the air. It swirled as a cloud around them. Their lights highlighted the particles. It was so thick they could barely see one another through it.

"Sarah, are you alright?" Beth said. "Are you hurt?"

Sarah cleared her throat. "I'm alive."

Their torch and headlamp beams flashed this way and that as everyone glanced around, choking on the dust, disoriented, shocked, frightened.

"Is everybody okay?" Juno asked in a muted panic. No one replied at first. "Is everyone okay?"

"Sure, I'm good," Holly said.

"Samantha?" Rebecca called out.

"Yeah, I'm good," Sam replied.

Hearing her voice, Rebecca reached out and grabbed her sister, pulling her closer to see more clearly.

"I'm really okay, Becca," Sam said firmly as she wormed out of her sister's grip.

Rebecca turned to Beth. "Are you okay?"

"Not by a long shot," Beth replied, keeping her eyes on Sarah, who was being helped to her feet by Juno.

"Everyone stay close until this dust settles," Juno said.

"We're not going anywhere," Sam replied.

"You're damn right about that," Holly added. She stared ahead at the fissure, her flashlight illuminating it.

Or—more precisely—where it used to be. The fissure was completely blocked up. Sealed by the rock collapse.

"No," Sam gasped as she looked at it.

Soon, all of them were standing around, staring at the fissure. Each of their headlamps shone upon it through the dust.

"So, what do we do?" Holly asked, trying to weigh the implications of what had happened.

"According to the guidebook," Rebecca replied, "this cave system has three ways in and out. This was just one of them. That right, Juno?"

Juno just turned away.

"Juno," Rebecca said again, "that's right, isn't it? Three? Can you check the book?"

Slowly and sheepishly, Juno turned back, awkwardness etched on her face. "I didn't bring the book down here."

"What?" Rebecca gasped.

"There's no point, is there?"

"Tell me you're kidding," Rebecca said, her voice turned sour.

"Why didn't you bring it?" Sam chimed in before quickly turning to her sister. "Why didn't she?"

While they quarrelled, Sarah slowly backed away from them and stared into the darkness in front of her, her flashlight barely breaking through it.

"For Christ's sake, Juno," Rebecca spat. "I knew it... I knew this wasn't right!"

"Oh, come on," Juno retorted. "This is what we've believed in for years! If there's no risk in any of it, what's the point? We may as well stay at home and watch fucking TV."

"Don't you try and justify this bullshit with your bravado!" Rebecca argued. "I know why you did this."

Behind them, Sarah swept her torch beam over the wall of the cavern, searching for an exit.

Searching for anything.

The dust from the collapse still hung thick in the air, masking what could be seen in the light—that was, until she moved her torch to one side. For a moment—a fraction of a second, from the corner of her eye—Sarah thought she saw something standing by the wall. Or someone. She darted her beam back to the spot and squinted through the heavy dust.

But there was nothing.

Again, nothing.

Looking around, she hoped her friends had seen it all, too. But they hadn't. They were all absorbed in arguments while Sarah quietly questioned her own mind.

"What are we going to do?" Sam pleaded to anyone who would answer.

"Don't fuckin' ask me." Holly shook her head. "This shit show isn't my doing."

"You filed a plan with Mountain Rescue, right? You said you would do that," Beth asked Rebecca frantically. "If we don't report in, they'll come looking for us, right?"

"Yeah. That's how it's supposed to work," Rebecca replied as she turned her attention to Juno with a furious glare. "Except I put the plan in for Boreham Caverns. But this isn't Boreham Caverns, is it, Juno?"

"We're in the wrong fucking caves?" Beth asked.

"You all wanted to go caving. Well, this is caving!" Juno protested. "Holly said it herself earlier. Boreham Caverns is nothing but a tourist trap."

"Don't try and pin this fuckin' shite on me."

"You all wanted adventure, didn't you? Well, this is it! This is the real thing!" Juno looked at each of them, wide-eyed, seeking validation but getting nothing but angry glares.

"This isn't caving, Juno," Rebecca said as she tried to calm her anger. "This is your ego trip... Your irresponsible, fucking dangerous ego trip!"

"So, where are we, then?" Sam asked in a panic.

"Yeah, where are we?" Rebecca added.

"It doesn't have a name. It's not in the books, anyway." Juno swallowed hard, the dust scratching her throat. "Nobody's been down here before, as far as I can tell. We're the first."

Sam whimpered. "Please, no."

"So, how do we get out?" Beth asked.

"I hate to be that asshole," Holly said matter-of-factly. "But there may not be a way out of here, right?"

Moving in suddenly, Beth squared up to Juno. "What the hell did you do?" she hissed. "What do you think this is going to do to us? To Sarah? How much more do you think she can take—not that you'd know what she's been through, because you couldn't get away fast enough, before!"

"You know what, Beth?" Juno said through gritted teeth. "We all lost something in that crash, alright? Get over it."

Beth paused, taken aback by this statement.

"Juno?" Sam asked. "You can get us out, right? You can do that, can't you?"

Juno spoke while she tried all she could to regain control. "We have to go on. Cave systems break ground every so often. There's a good chance that there could be an exit out in the next cave. But we won't know unless we carry on. Because if we just stay here, we'll die. Simple as that. Is that plain enough for everyone?" She took a breath. "Now, I made some decisions that cannot be undone. There is no point fighting about it now. Not here. It won't change a thing. So, let's just move on and focus on getting out, okay?"

Without another word, they each grabbed the gear they had set down and prepared to move on.

Sarah still stood motionless and apart from the rest, staring into the darkness, hoping for another glimpse of whatever or whomever she'd glimpsed through the dust. It couldn't all be in her head. She was sane. She was. She was. Maybe Juno had seen something.

"Juno," she called out quietly.

"What is it?" Juno replied, agitated.

Sarah shook her head. "Actually, never mind... It's nothing. It has to be nothing."

"I promise you, Sarah," Juno said, "I'm gonna get us all out of here, okay? I promise."

Chapter 7

THE CHASM

The cavern opened up before them. The walls on each side were slick with moisture, shimmering under their headlights and torches. Water droplets steadily dripped down from the low ceiling—a rhythmic tap, tap, tap, like the tick of a countdown, echoing around them.

The air felt colder the farther down they went, a bitter, deathly cold, sharp enough to claw at their lungs and leave the unsettling taste of staleness.

Beneath their feet, the rock sloped into darkness and Juno led the way. Picking her foot placement carefully over the uneven decline, she took every step with a measured gamble. As her weight came down, the loose smattering of stones on top shifted and cracked under her heel. When she glanced back towards the others, her pale headlamp passed over their worried faces. Each was as pale and nervous as the next, and each stared at her in judgement.

As Juno's pace slowed, Sam cut ahead of her, urgently wanting to find an exit.

"Sam!" Rebecca suddenly screamed. "Don't move!"

Her voice reverberated around the chamber as if it was on loudspeaker, so loud it shattered the haunting soundtrack of their shallow breaths and the relentless tap, tap, tap.

Sam stopped dead in her tracks, shocked by her sister's sudden command. As was everyone else.

"Wh-What?" Sam asked weakly, not turning back. Not even blinking. Not daring to budge.

"Just stay right where you are," Rebecca added.

Juno, reaching into the small pack on her back, removed another phosphorus flare. Removing the cap, she ignited it in one swift motion. As the bright glow billowed out, the cavern was bathed in a flickering light. A beam that clearly showed the ground dropping away only a few inches from where Sam stood. A drop that fell straight down into a large ravine, stretching about twenty feet across. The bottom of which could not be seen.

With the ceiling only a couple of feet above their heads, they stood at the very top of the gorge.

"Shit!" Sam gasped and scrambled backwards, her eyes locked on the void ahead.

The group froze in shock.

Even Juno had gasped. She should have been looking out for this while she was leading them. She should have seen it, since it was just in front of her.

Holding the flare up high, she turned to Sam, wanting to say sorry.

Beth picked up a stone by her feet, carefully stepped over to the edge, and tossed it over.

Everyone paused. A long pause.

Then a distant clatter, as the rock collided with the ravine floor.

"Thanks for that." Rebecca shook her head as she peered over. "Now I know it's a damn long way down."

"Huh? I just copied what you did back at the entrance. Thought you could tell how deep it was from that?"

"That's for going down. We're gonna go across. And that someone is me." Rebecca sighed. "I'd rather have not known how far down it went. As would most people. Fear can't play into any of it."

"Wait, why you?" Beth asked. "I thought Juno was the best at climbing?"

"It's not a question of skill," Juno cut in. "Rebecca has the longest reach and is much stronger than me. You'd rather someone like her do this." With that, she stepped up and scanned the chasm. "Over there." She pointed to one darker part of the opposite wall.

With that, she tossed her flare over the gap, where it smacked against the far rock then landed on the opposite ledge. Its burning illumination highlighted a cleft in the rock face just to the left on the edge. "That's maybe the way we need to go."

"Maybe?" Holly asked.

"It's all maybe," Juno replied. "Nothing's for sure."

Rebecca swept her gaze across the ravine from left to right, her torch following her gaze. Then she turned to the ceiling above, squinting as she examined it.

"Looking good?" Juno asked.

"What does it matter?" Rebecca turned to her with a blank expression. "There's no alternative, is there?"

Ignoring the attitude justifiably aimed at her, Juno joined her in staring up at the ceiling. "There's a crack," she said, pointing to a thin crevice. "Running right across."

"I see it," Rebecca said. "Yeah, that'll do. I can use that."

"How do you use it?" Sam asked.

"I have to get over there freestyle so I can rig some line for you guys to cross over. One traverse line and one safety." Rebecca pointed to the part of the ceiling with the crack. "So, I gotta go hand over hand, gripping in any cracks in the rock, and hang the hell on while I fix it all up for you."

"You've done this before?" Beth asked worriedly.

"No, but I saw a guy do it once on an artificial wall, over some crash mats." Once Beth's expression turned to grave concern, Rebecca smiled. "I'm kidding! Like Juno said, I got a lot of experience."

But this did little to ease everyone's nerves as they stared at Rebecca with a mixture of hope and fear. All except for Juno, who was rigging one end of a safety rope to a climbing piton jammed into the wall behind them.

"Well, fortune favours the bold." Rebecca shrugged and took out a pair of heavy leather gloves from her pocket. She slid them on. "Let's just get this done."

Her words were full of businesslike confidence. Emotionless yet certain.

Juno attached the coil of the safety rope to Rebecca's harness. "Got enough cams?" She stared at the cams hanging from her belt.

Rebecca just nodded as she stared at the ceiling, studying the path.

After flexing her fists and quickly shaking them out, Rebecca stepped over to a part of the ceiling beneath the crack that traced across the gap. She jammed her fingers in between the split rock. Clenching and without a pause, she then swung her feet off the floor to test its weight before moving out over the drop.

"Looks good," she said aloud to herself, still hanging by all her weight.

"Please be careful," Sam said with a tremble in her voice.

Sarah, meanwhile, stood quietly at the back of the group. She watched them all while she listened to the tap, tap, tap of the drips around her.

With a smile, Rebecca swung her body forward and reached out over the drop, then thrust her fingers into the next part of the crack along the ceiling. Gripping onto the fissure with all her strength, she let go with her other hand, removed a spring-loaded cam that hung from her belt, and wedged it forcefully into the crack.

She was directly over the drop. Directly over the very deep, terrifying drop.

Sam watched fearfully, expecting the worst. "Please, please, please," she whispered. Praying.

Juno, noticing Sam, spoke assuredly while she kept her eyes on Rebecca. "Those are cams she's putting in the rock. Rebecca will now hook her safety line onto it, so she's safe as can be at every step of the climb."

Rebecca grabbed the line from her belt that led back to

Juno and hooked it onto the cam she'd just fixed.

"See?" Juno added to Sam. "Worst part over. She's attached to that line as well. So, she's also secured."

Without pause, Rebecca reached forward again, not looking down at all, and gripped the next part of the crack above her. After attaching another cam, she hooked her line to it and moved on.

Swapping her weight from one hand to the other, she reached out and thrust her hand into a further part of the crack. Each time she moved forward, she removed a cam from her belt, placed it in the ceiling, and hooked the line through it.

One by one, she slowly edged her way along towards the ledge on the far side.

Beth glanced at Juno, who was focused on Rebecca, gripping her safety line tight in her hands, ready to act at a moment's notice.

Sam just stared on helplessly.

Holly reached up and grabbed the camcorder from the mount on her helmet. Hitting the record button, she hoped to capture this despite the low light.

Sarah still stared on silently.

Passing the halfway point across the ravine, Rebecca stopped dead in her tracks, eyes widening. Her gaze as fixed on something sticking out of the ceiling.

Noticing the delay, Juno called out, "Anything wrong?"

Above Rebecca, jammed into the crack, was a climbing piton. A very old one.

"Uh, nothing," Rebecca replied. "Just a quick rest!"

Knowing there was no time to waste dwelling on unnecessary questions as to why the piton was there, Rebecca swung herself just beyond it. Then she turned, grabbed a carabiner off one of the cams, and attached it to the old piton. With speed, she hooked the line through it.

Waste not, want not, she thought to herself.

Below her, though, Rebecca could feel the pull of the deep. The gravity of the darkness beneath seemed stronger than anywhere else, like the very chasm itself was trying to grab at her.

Two more swings, two more cams placed, two more points where the safety line was affixed, and Rebecca reached the opposite ledge. Dropping down to her feet in the dirt beside the flare, she smiled happily at her friends across the drop.

"How does the exit look?" Juno called out.

Rebecca peered at the tall but narrow gap in the rock to her left, just big enough to squeeze through. "Dark."

Her attention was then drawn back to the old piton in the ceiling. *Whoever has been here*, she thought, *must have gone through this way.*

But that could be either the best or the worst thing to happen. They could either have made it out, or climbed through here to their doom.

She shook it off and turned to Juno. "Throw me the line."

Juno hurled the coiled line across to Rebecca while keeping hold of one end. It unfurled as it flew, and Rebecca leaned out over the bottomless drop and grasped the flailing end of the rope.

From her belt, she removed a piton and turned to the wall, searching for a place to secure it. Noticing a perfect small crack, she jammed the piton in, its teeth gripping onto the rock. Then she tied the line to it.

All this was done very calmly and expertly. Despite the myriad intrusive thoughts in her mind screaming about worst-case scenarios, Rebecca had pushed them all down and just did what she had to do.

"Alright, who's first?" she called out to her friends.

The secured rope went taut as Juno fixed the other end.

Without thinking about it twice, Sam stepped up. "I'll go."

Juno clipped Sam's harness to the now-taut traverse line. "This one will hold your weight, okay?" Juno explained while she attached a second harness to the first line that ran across the ceiling via the cams. "And you pull yourself across on this safety line." She pointed to the first cam. "And at each section, at each cam you come to, reach up and unclip your harness. Move it just in front of the cam and pull yourself on the traverse line to the next one. Keep repeating till you're at the other side. Easy, huh?"

With a nod, Sam walked forward and grabbed the safety rope across the ceiling.

"Just lean back slowly," Juno added. "The ropes can hold ten of you. They're really strong."

Sam remembered doing this years ago. She closed her eyes and held the safety line tightly, then lowered herself backwards over the drop. Not thinking of the chasm she was about to crawl across.

The tension line held her weight, and after a few seconds she bent to pull herself over the first section of the line.

"Now, reach up and move your harness to the other side of the cam," Rebecca called out.

Sam remembered what to do but still appreciated the commentary from both her sister and Juno. She needed all the assurances she could get.

Reaching up, Sam unclipped her harness.

"Good," Juno called out. "Now, just reclip it ahead."

Within a couple of minutes, Sam had made it across.

Rebecca reached out and pulled her over to the ledge with a smile. "You make it look easy! Show-off."

"Piece of cake," Sam replied with a nervous laugh.

Holly was up next, and she crossed the gap smoothly without a word spoken by anyone.

Then it was Beth's turn. No one noticed the piton in the wall behind Rebecca that started to jar as Beth pulled her weight across it.

Next up was Sarah.

Juno clipped her onto the traverse and safety lines, then offered her a smile. "It'll be easy."

Sarah nodded, her worry evident.

As she pulled herself across the halfway point, the traverse line piton behind Rebecca started to shift again. Each time she pulled her weight along the traverse line, it caused the piton to loosen incrementally.

It was not long before Sarah reached the other side, where Rebecca pulled her to safety next to Beth, Sam, and

Holly. They stood in front of the cleft in the wall—their potential exit.

Back on the other side, Juno was already hooked up by her harnesses and began to make her way across the chasm. Without an ounce of concern or trepidation, she moved fast. She had done this a hundred times before, and that was evident.

Sarah, who was standing behind Beth, peered into the cleft behind her. Into the darkness that her headlamp did little to break through. She stared into it as if daring the dark to make a noise.

But her attention was immediately jolted away when the piton behind Rebecca broke free of its mooring with a loud crack. Juno yelped.

Rebecca, having been gripping the traverse line for extra safety, suddenly had to take Juno's full weight. The rope drew back rapidly, its friction burning through her leather glove like butter and lacerating her palm. Blood gushed out as the smell of burning flesh hit her nostrils.

"Juno!" Sarah screamed as Rebecca cried out in agony, still trying to grip the rope through her wound.

Beth and Sam lunged forward and grabbed hold of the traverse line, taking the weight off Rebecca.

But before they could stop Juno's fall, the safety line kicked in and her body was short-stopped with a jolt, suspending her in midair from the waist.

Hanging there, Juno looked up to the safety line and noticed the very old piton holding her.

A piton giving way and coming free from the rock.

"No!" Juno yelled out as the old piton dislodged and her body quickly dropped another two feet down and jolted hard once the other cams secured her weight again.

She dangled there like a broken marionette, trying to focus through her panic.

Sam and Beth held the traverse line tightly.

"It's alright," Beth called out. "We got you!"

Juno could only look up in bemusement as the old piton slid down the safety line towards her. She reached up and grabbed it. The light from her helmet shone over its rough surface. Turning back to the ledge, she could see Rebecca crying, cradling her palm.

Sarah and Holly joined Sam and Beth at the traverse line and, with all their might, pulled Juno over to the ledge.

Once Juno was safely across, Sam rushed over to Rebecca's side to attend to her hand. Using a small medical kit from her backpack, Sam carefully removed the remnants of Rebecca's glove from around the gouge in her palm.

Juno, panicked but masking it as best as she could, grasped the old piton. After removing it from the safety line, she held it out to Sarah.

"What's this?" Sarah asked as she peered down at the old metal.

Standing beside her, Beth stared at it, too.

"Means we're not the first here," Juno replied.

"Is that good?" Beth said, hopefully.

"Possibly." Juno shrugged. "But this equipment's old. No one uses stuff like this anymore."

"Maybe they never made it out?" Sarah mused.

Behind them, Rebecca moaned as Sam wrapped a bandage tightly around her hand.

"The rope cauterised a lot of the wound," Sam said. "I managed to stop the rest of the bleeding for now. But you were lucky."

"Rebecca, you feel okay?" Juno asked.

Rebecca managed a pained smile as she tried to close her fist, but she could hardly move it without causing a shooting pain. "I'll live."

After a few minutes of rest, they carried on through the cleft in the rock. Through the narrow passage, they found themselves at the mouth of a winding, narrow tunnel.

Holly walked on ahead, checking out what was to come.

As the group walked, a sense of intense trepidation surrounded them. They had narrowly escaped a tragedy but were not left unscathed. Each felt an intense urgency to escape.

"Holly?" Juno called out. "How does it look up there?"

Farther up the tunnel, beyond a sharp bend, Holly's voice came echoing back. "It's tight through here, but it soon opens out."

"Alright, just keep going," Juno replied. "Watch your step. We'll be right behind you."

The group turned the corner and through a tight gap in the rock, one that led to a strange-looking angular cavern.

Holly was first to see it and stared ahead, her torch and headlamp shining. "Hey! There's something in here."

One by one, the others squeezed themselves from the narrow tunnel into this new space.

Holly gazed up, wide-eyed. As each of the others entered, they joined her. Standing by her side, staring in wonderment.

Their lights traced over the large flat wall that stretched high up. A wall littered with cave paintings.

Their beams shone over fragments of the large image. Crude drawings of figures hunting animals—figures on all fours—all in front of a large cave mouth. To the right of it was the same sketch, the same open cave, but this time with different figures in front of it. Figures of all sizes. Large and small.

Beth took a cautious step closer, fascinated by the images. Studying them in closer detail, she alternated her beam across both sets of drawings. "It's like a mirror painting: two images, but they're one?"

"What is this? History class, Beth?" Juno said. "We got bigger fish to fry than a few drawings."

Beth's eyes widened and she smiled. "Wait a minute!" She backed up, looking around at the bigger picture.

"Beth?" Rebecca said. "What is it?"

Beth didn't answer her, too caught up in her thoughts. Realising something, she turned to Juno. "Hey, light up one of the flares."

"What? Why?"

"Just light a fucking flare," Beth snapped.

Juno looked at Beth in silent shock.

"Please?" Beth added, dropping the anger. "Just light one. Now."

Reluctantly, yet wanting to avoid any more

confrontation, Juno unclipped a flare from her belt, removed its cap, and lit it.

As the white glow filled the room, Beth's smile returned. "Look at that beautiful bastard. What do you see?"

"Lots of drawings?" Holly guessed.

"No—well, yes, but no." Beth glanced at her. "It's one big painting. It's the whole damn place, it's the forest, the cave—or should I say caves?"

Everyone gazed up at the drawings and noticed one pointed shape encompassing all of them—the mountain. There were trees drawn in a darker shade, only noticeable by the flare's light.

"Two entrances joined together," Beth added.

They all scanned the drawing. The two cave entrances sat side by side among the trees, with a line between them.

"Beth, you're a fucking genius!" Rebecca said.

"Then, there's a way out?" Sam added.

"Let's find out." Sarah smiled.

A renewed hope flooded through each of them, a hope that eclipsed the dread.

Chapter 8

THE STREAM

Holding the burning flare out in front of her, Juno led the way through a high-ceilinged, winding tunnel. The others followed at a fast pace in a huddle.

The tunnel went on, twisting and turning, inclining and declining. So much so that any sense of direction they might have had was soon forgotten.

Around a blind bend to the left, Juno's confident march was suddenly halted and she was forced to stop dead in her tracks. The rest had no choice but to follow suit.

"Shit," Juno hissed. "Shit, shit, shit."

They stared as the tunnel opened and split into three different directions.

"We need a lighter," Juno added as she turned to the group. "Anyone got one? Or matches?"

"Finally, I can be useful!" Holly said with a smirk, quickly whipping out a neon-pink lighter.

Juno took it and approached the first tunnel.

"You need a smoke?" Holly asked.

Juno didn't answer, but Rebecca spoke up.

"Best way to find an exit is to see if there's a breeze coming down it. No breeze means no exit."

"Ah, gotcha," Holly replied.

Juno held up the lighter flame to the first tunnel and studied it.

No breeze. The flame burnt perfectly still.

Then she moved over to the second tunnel without saying a word, and held up the flame again.

Nothing. No movement.

"Damn," she said and took a quick breath in.

Dread crept in as a thought raced around her mind: What if none of the tunnels have a breeze?

She moved over to the last tunnel, lit the lighter, and held her breath.

It flickered inward.

Juno smiled, relieved. Finally, some luck!

"Guess that's the one, then," Holly said. She stepped forward, sped past Juno, and walked down the tunnel.

"Holly, wait!" Juno said. "Dammit, Holly." She grimaced as the rest of the group took off down the third tunnel.

Holly was hurrying ahead. She had heard Juno but just didn't want to stop. As she rushed down the tunnel, something caught her eye.

Quickly flicking off her helmet light and torch, she glimpsed something in the pitch darkness, her heart skipping a beat. A faint glow reflected off the wall.

"Daylight! I see daylight!"

Rushing forward, not waiting for the group and without

bothering to switch her torch back on, she ran towards the light.

The corner bent and Holly rushed around it, but her face contorted in horror once she saw there was no daylight. Instead, algae was growing all over the walls, creating a luminescent glow. She tried to slow down, but slipped on the moss where the floor gave way into a rocky sinkhole. Losing control, she slid down an uneven rock face covered in the same moist, luminescent algae.

Juno appeared around the corner and launched herself onto the floor at the edge of the sinkhole. Reaching her arm forward, she grasped for Holly but, in doing so, slammed her arm against a sharp rock. She winced but held out her hand.

"Help me!" Holly screamed, reaching up for Juno.

Their hands met and Juno tried to grip it as tightly as possible, but the slime from the algae on Holly's hands made it impossible to keep a firm hold. Holly's weight pulled at her arm and pressed it harder into the sharp rock, which had broken through the skin.

"Please," Holly cried as her fingers slipped from Juno's.

"Don't move!"

Holly's fingers pulled from Juno's grasp. She yelped and slid down the slimy rock, slowly but inexorably, into the sinkhole below. A sinkhole that funnelled as it descended, constricting narrower and narrower.

Holly could only look up in horror, and Juno stared back helplessly.

As she slid down, she did not notice the many deep scratch marks littering the walls that closed in.

Sarah and the others reached the edge of the sinkhole just in time to see Holly's terrified face disappearing over the brink.

"No!" Sam screamed.

Soon after she disappeared from view, but before anyone could say anything, a dull thud hit the ground, followed by a loud moan.

"Holly?" Juno called out.

In the darkness of the chamber she had fallen into, Holly lay helpless in a heap, slowly coming to after a brief spell of unconsciousness.

"Holly?" she heard Juno calling out, sounding far away.

She became aware of a sharp pain tracing up her leg. She lifted her head and realised she lay in a flow of shallowly running water. An underground stream ran past her.

"Shit," she groaned, her voice filled with annoyance. Her shaking fingers reached down towards her leg, where a sharp, throbbing pain radiated up her thigh.

Agony began to intensify and it pulsed in time with her heartbeats, twisting deeper into her nerves with each passing throb. Her hand, still slick with algae, blindly explored her lower leg until her fingers brushed against something hard, foreign—wrong.

Her breath hitched as she traced over a jagged edge of bone jutting through her shin.

"Holly, please say something?"

Juno's voice came again, more distant, muffled by the roaring pain in Holly's ears.

"I think I... I hurt my leg," Holly rasped.

The sharp ache made it impossible to breathe deeply.

She clawed at the dark headlamp on her helmet, fumbling to turn it on with her trembling fingers.

The beam of light flickered to life and cut through the shadow to land on her leg. Her stomach churned as she saw the damage, and a wave of nausea threatened to pull her under. She bit down hard on her lip, forcing herself to stay conscious.

Her shinbone, splintered and pale, pierced through torn, blood-streaked flesh. The skin had been peeled back in a ragged flap and the insides glistened in the harsh light. There wasn't much blood—at least, not as much as she expected—but what was there clung in thick, black-red smears. The real horror was in the exposed muscle and sinew that stretched grotesquely around the bone like shredded fabric.

The nausea intensified, as did the pain. Her hands shook uncontrollably where they hovered uselessly above the wound.

She couldn't touch it. She couldn't stop the pain. She was helpless.

Holly gasped, on the verge of tears. "Please, get down here."

High above her, Juno was already at work, ignoring the cut on her arm that bled down to her elbow. She and Rebecca were hammering pitons into the rock. After they were secure, they grabbed ropes from around their shoulders and tied them on, getting ready to abseil down.

"Sam," Juno said as she finished tying a clove hitch, "you go first. You got your medical bag?"

Sam nodded but she gave Rebecca a worried look.

"You'll be fine," Rebecca said, cradling her throbbing hand.

"We have to move you," Sam said, crouched beside Holly. "And I warn you now, it's gonna hurt like a son of a bitch."

"Alright," Holly said through gritted teeth. "Please make it quick... make it quick, quick, quick. I don't wanna feel this any more than I have to."

"How is it?" Sarah asked, peering over Sam's shoulder at the wound on Holly's leg.

"There's no arterial damage from what I can see. In no time, the bleeding should stop. These things usually look way worse than they are. But I need to have a closer look before we move her. Just in case." Taking a clasp knife from her belt, Sam leaned forward and cut open Holly's trouser leg, revealing the true extent of the injury to everyone.

"Ah, god!" Beth exclaimed. "That's fucking disgusting!"

"Holly, why the hell did you run ahead?" Juno asked as she stared down at the bloody wound. "You can't go do stuff like that. We have to stick together!"

Holly grimaced in agony but she nodded. "I know... You play stupid games, you get stupid prizes, I guess," she said. "Can't get more stupider than this."

"Guys," Sam chided. "Not here. Not now. Now, help me. All of you. She's good to move over to that rock, as long as we're careful. So, help me move her out of this water."

Holly was fast becoming delirious with the pain.

Rebecca, Juno, and Beth gathered around her while Sam cradled the broken leg as gently as she could. "Nice and easy now... lift."

Holly groaned loudly as they lifted her out of the stream and moved her over to a large rocky ledge.

"Ahh, Jeeessussss," Holly screamed.

"Juno," Sam said urgently, "pass me the first aid kit. And see if you can find something to make a splint from."

Rebecca stared at Sam proudly for the first time, seeing her sister in her element, and felt a newfound admiration.

Looking in her pack, Beth pulled out a spare T-shirt, folded it, and crouched beside Holly, placing it under her head as a makeshift pillow.

Juno grabbed Holly's bag and withdrew the pick. Unscrewing the blade, she inspected the handle and nodded to herself. "That'll do."

While Sam tried her best to clean and dress Holly's leg wound, Rebecca activated snap lights and placed them around. They filled the cavern with a soft blue glow.

Sarah drifted backwards from the others.

Her concentration was being dragged away by the strange noises around the cave. Noises no one else seemed to pay any attention to. She wanted to ask everyone if they could hear them, too, but the thought they might say no was devastating. Even though she knew these noises were probably in her mind, imagining everyone looking at her even more pityingly than they did already—well, that was something she had to avoid. But she needed to know for herself.

Farther up the stream, she could hear the faintest of sounds, a light clacking she could not quite place. Rocks falling, maybe? She stepped closer, curious.

Rebecca, Beth, and Sam were crowded around Holly's leg while she moaned quietly, paying no attention to the strange sounds.

Rebecca looked at Beth and Sam in turn. "This is the second time that one of you rushed ahead of us." She motioned to Holly's leg. "This is bad, yeah, but could've been way worse. So, please. Let Juno or me lead at all times."

Sam nodded guiltily, knowing she had almost fallen to her death not that long ago—and also for running ahead. Forgetting that this place was not safe.

Juno turned and saw Sarah step away. "Sarah, don't wander off! Sarah?"

Rebecca shook her head and muttered, "What did I just fucking say?"

"Guys," Sam said, "I need your help here."

But Juno still stared at Sarah, who was slowly walking away.

"Juno," Sam shouted, tearing Juno's attention back. "Take hold of her arm. You're all going to need to hold her down."

"What are you gonna do?" Holly asked weakly.

Sam looked down at her with a small smile. "I need to dress the wound and rig up a splint, but I can't do that while the bone is sticking out. So, I..." She shrugged apologetically. "I have to push it back."

Holly's eyes opened wide in shock, but knowing she

had no choice, she just lay her head back onto the T-shirt pillow, trembling.

"Here, bite down on this," Sam said, placing a leather strap from Holly's rucksack between her teeth.

Rebecca held down the other leg, with Beth and Juno on her arms.

"Try to hold her still," Sam said. "Movement can make it worse."

Holly, petrified, bit down hard on the strap, trying to focus.

Beth shut her eyes, unable to watch as Sam pried open the muscles in Holly's leg with her fingers, then used her thumb to force the bone back in.

Her biting down on the strap did little as Holly let out a blood-curdling scream.

Though Sarah heard Holly's screams, she continued to walk upstream in a daze, pacing deeper and deeper into the network of watery tunnels.

Just up ahead, her torch caught an object sticking out of the water on a rock. Something metal. She approached it, and the beam of her light reflected off its silver surface.

Picking it up, she quickly recognised the object as a badly damaged old miner's helmet with a large, ragged hole in its side. The sharp edges of the hole frayed inward. Painted letters on the front of the helmet came into view. Oswald.

Before she could examine it further, another noise from upstream grabbed her attention. A bird squawking, maybe? An injured animal?

*

With one last push, after two failed attempts, Sam finally managed to set the bone back into place. Through the searing pain, Holly gasped for air as tears streamed down her cheeks.

"I'm sorry," she sobbed.

"Pass me the splint," Sam asked Juno, holding her hand out expectantly.

Juno nodded and placed the pick handle in her grasp, though she kept an eye towards the direction Sarah had walked off in.

"After all this, she just walked off." Rebecca shook her head, glancing upstream.

"We should go get her," Beth added.

Absently turning the helmet over, Sarah felt a sudden chill. The stream around her feet had begun to soak through her boots.

She stared ahead, tilting her head from side to side and allowing the beam of light from her helmet to sweep from left to right ahead of her. The torch in her hand followed.

Then something vague caught her eye as her beam slid over it in the distance. Whatever it was, it was paler than the dark rock surrounding it.

Slowing her pace, she aimed her light directly ahead at the object. The closer she got, the more form it took, yet it somehow remained indistinguishable.

Sarah blinked hard and began to doubt herself. Was there even anything there? If she got there and she had imagined it, she knew she had no choice left. She would have to tell the others.

She took a few more steps and prayed for what she was seeing to be real. But then the shape moved slightly, causing her to freeze in her tracks.

Sarah took very slow, very cautious steps closer. As she did, the shape took on a more definite form.

A form that made her freeze. A form that made her hold her breath in fear. A form that made her wish it was just in her head.

It was a figure.

Human, maybe?

It faced away, squatting low, hunched on a rock. Its head and shoulders moved slightly, and the slurping of water could be heard over the trickling stream.

She didn't know what to do. She was stuck, staring at it.

I'm not losing my mind. It's real.

Then its head jolted upward as it turned to the side. Listening for something. Alerted.

She could not determine much about what this thing was but could tell it was incredibly gaunt and sinewy, naked, and sickeningly pale. If it were a wild animal, it had no fur. If it was a human, it was a distorted version of one.

A sudden hand grasping her shoulder caused Sarah to jolt backwards and spin, almost blinding Juno with her headlamp.

"Sarah, what the hell are you doing?" Juno said. "Everyone needs to stop walking off. This is not safe here—you get that, right?"

"T-There's something." Sarah tried to peer back over her shoulder. "I saw something. A man... up ahead in the tunnel. On that rock." Turning back, she aimed her torch to where the thing was.

"Well, there's nothing there," Juno said. "You must've imagined it."

Sarah, without looking away, handed Juno the miner's helmet. "I'm imagining a lot down here," she muttered. "But this is real."

Sarah turned and headed back down the tunnel to the others, leaving Juno holding the helmet.

Sam had finished dressing Holly's wound and strapped the pick handle to her leg as a rudimentary splint.

More lucid now, Holly sat on the edge of the rock with her legs dangling off.

Still in pain. Still exhausted. Still scared. But much better.

"There," Sam said, admiring the wound dressing. "That's the best I can do down here. It'll hurt like hell, and you won't be able to put much weight on it, but you can move."

Holly nodded and slowly lowered her leg to the floor, wincing with pain.

"It's just old mining gear, Sarah. Who cares?" Juno said as she and Sarah returned to the group, obviously in the middle of an animated discussion. "They combed these mountains for gold over a half-century ago! Anyone trapped down here would be a skeleton by now. Not making a home."

Sarah stared at the floor as she walked and spoke quietly. "That's just what it looked like, that's all I'm saying. I think it was real. It had to be."

“What what looked like?” Beth asked.

Juno shook her head. “Sarah thinks she saw somebody back there.”

“She what?” Beth said, turning to Sarah. “You did?”

“I don’t think I saw someone. I saw someone. I did.”

Exasperated, Juno spoke louder. “You heard something and then you saw what you wanted to see. It’s the dark down here. It plays tricks on you.”

Beth silently thought the same thing while she regarded Sarah with concern.

“There are things I want to see, Juno,” Sarah said sadly. “That wasn’t one of them.”

“So, what did you see, then?” Sam asked.

“Don’t encourage her,” Juno said.

“A man. I saw a man.”

“Are you sure?” Rebecca said.

Sarah shrugged. “I think, and it’s not the first time. I saw someone down here before. I kept hearing things. Clicking and scraping. But now I’m sure I saw that.” Glancing around, she saw five doubtful faces staring back at her. “Really, I saw it.”

Juno caught Beth’s eye. A mutual look of worry lingered between them.

“Sarah,” Juno said, her voice softer, “whether there is or isn’t someone down here, you have to forget it. We have one thing to concentrate on: getting out and getting Holly to a hospital. That is the most important thing. Agreed?”

Sarah could not argue.

“What if I am imagining it?”

*

Juno stared at the lighter's flame as it flickered away from her, farther down the tunnel. Walking against the flow of the stream that ran beneath them, she pointed ahead. "This is the way." She, Rebecca, and Sarah led the way.

Behind them, Holly was propped up by Beth and Sam, hopping along in pain. Each movement sent a fresh jolt of agony from her shin up through her body.

Through various twists and turns, their journey up the tunnel was cold and slow. Eventually, they reached the head of the stream and a small waterfall, where the water fell from the next chamber above.

Juno stepped forward and was the first to peer up over the edge of the waterfall into the higher chamber. She expected to see another dark expanse, much like the dozens they had already crossed through, nothing out of the ordinary. In her wildest dreams, she would have hoped to see daylight, that they would soon step into the fresh air again.

Juno did not see what she expected or what she dreamed.

Her eyes widened in sickened shock.

Chapter 9
THE BONE DAM

Thin streams of water tumbled down from multiple points across the high chamber's ceiling. The water did not flow freely, though, as it flooded the chamber in nearly two feet of water, blocked at the mouth of the small waterfall by a large obstruction. Choked by something grotesque.

A large dam had formed at the end of the chamber that slowed the water's flow. Not made of stone nor branches nor other debris from the outside world, however: this dam was a blockade made from broken animal bones, twisted together like a grotesque web.

Water could only trickle through cracks in the dam between the masses of bones in a steady leak of what was, by the time it made its way to the tunnels below, quite stagnant.

Standing on top of the bone dam, having crawled over the crest of the waterfall, all six women stared down at the macabre sight before them.

Among the tangle of remains beneath their feet, something caught Sarah's eye—shreds of fabric, tangled and torn, caught on the jagged ends of some animal carcass. The material looked old and faded, barely recognisable as anything specific.

Maybe they belonged to the miner, Oswald? she thought to herself. Maybe that thing I saw was Oswald?

She scanned for evidence of human remains, but there was none. No human skulls, no human bones.

"What is this?" Beth asked, not wanting to hear an answer.

"Looks like a slaughterhouse," Sam mused. She felt sick, staring at the mass of bones at her feet.

"Holly?" Sarah said. "Can I borrow your camcorder? I want to see this place in infrared."

Holly reached up and unclasped the camera from her helmet, then handed it to Sarah. "It's called 'night shot' on there. Just turn the dial at the top to the symbol of the moon."

After fumbling with the controls, Sarah activated the night shot infrared function which, on the viewfinder, displayed the whole cavern in a bright green hue.

Scanning ahead, Sarah stared at the many piles of bones littered around the space, bunching up in small piles that breached the water like islands—part of a deathly archipelago.

"So many animals," she said. "Hundreds. Thousands. Why?"

Juno turned her torch to the rest of the chamber around them, shining her light over the walls. Along its dark stone, she could occasionally see darker patches where tunnels led off to other parts of the cave system.

Beth shook her head and mumbled, "This definitely can't be good."

Nervously, Sam turned to Rebecca. "Can we just keep going? I don't want to stay in here."

Rebecca called over to Juno. "Which way you wanna go?"

"One sec," Juno said as she took out the lighter. But as she ignited the flame, it billowed in all directions, as if the wind came from every tunnel here. "I don't know," she said, shaken.

Sarah aimed the infrared around them, scanning all the walls and floor.

"What do you mean you don't know?" Beth asked.

Juno shrugged. "The breeze is coming from all over the place. It could be any one of these tunnels around here. Take your pick."

"Doesn't that mean there's an exit at the end of all of them?" Beth asked.

"No, the wind from one could be part of the wind from another. It just means that there are a lot of connected tunnels."

"Hello?" Rebecca called out across the cavern. "Is anybody there?"

Juno shook her head. "Oh, please."

Sarah caught Beth in the shot as she stepped forward. Through the ghostly haze of the night-vision lens, her face was eerie and pale, glowing against the shadowy backdrop. Her eyes appeared luminous and unnaturally bright, reflecting the infrared light like beams from her sockets.

"Right now, right here, I'm willing to try anything." Beth turned to face the cavern. "Hello?"

Her voice reverberated around them.

Sarah angled the camera onto Juno, who looked annoyed. Then Rebecca and Beth called out across the chamber again.

When the lens returned to look at Beth, she was not alone.

Sarah gasped. She stared at the viewfinder.

Just behind Beth, another figure loomed over her. Vaguely human and paler than Beth in the green of the infrared. Hairless and gaunt, with eyes that appeared to be sealed closed. It had large, mutated ears tipped into a bat-like point, and a distended jawline to accommodate a mouthful of jagged teeth.

As its mouth opened, Sarah could not keep the words from escaping.

"Beth, behind you!" she screamed, looking up from the viewfinder while Beth reeled in terror.

Juno's torch beam turned on Beth, but the pale figure had retreated into the shadows, scuttering up the walls and growling low. A clicking, guttural snarl faded away and its claws scraped up the stone walls.

"What the fuck was that?" Beth shouted. All their torches flashed frantically around the chamber.

Their beams spun while they tried to find where the creature had gone. But it was too fast, darting left and right, up and across the walls and ceiling, evading every one of their attempts to locate it. Its growls continued until, from the far end of the chamber, it let loose a hideously piercing shriek.

In a panic, Juno struggled to light a flare quickly enough. By the time she did and cast the whole cavern into flickering light, the thing, this creature, this crawler, had left.

"Jesus!" Holly exclaimed.

"What was that?" Beth shouted. "What the fuck was that?"

"I don't know," Rebecca said, scanning the walls, struggling to regulate her breathing. "I couldn't really see. It moved so fast!"

"Juno, I told you we weren't alone," Sarah said.

"Sarah," Sam shouted, "that was not a fucking miner. That was not a fucking human being!"

"Fuck it," Juno said as she gritted her teeth, steadying herself. "Let's just pick a tunnel and take our chances. That thing ran when we made a noise. If it comes back, we'll do the same again. Scream at it. Scare it off."

Beth, propping Holly up, nodded to the nearest tunnel to the right, fewer than ten feet away. "Let's try that way first?" she suggested, then turned to Holly. "You good?"

Holly nodded. "All good."

With the rest close behind, they walked into the tunnel. After they'd moved about a dozen paces deeper, everyone came to a shocked stop as the terrible rasping screech came from far down the tunnel before them.

"Make some noise," Juno said.

They all began to scream in anger at the tops of their lungs. Screaming down the tunnel to ward off the beast.

As their voices faded, they glanced at each other, assuming they had scared the thing off. But then a shriek came at them again.

This time, it was closer.

Without needing to say a word, all six of them backed away, each thinking the same thing. This wasn't the tunnel they wanted to walk down.

As they rushed through the next tunnel, Beth propped up Holly in front, with Juno right behind them while she held on to the hissing flare. They moved as fast as they could in a stagger. They passed many clefts in the rocks that led to other chambers, but they decided to keep heading straight.

They could still hear the creature's calls ringing out in furious, animalistic cries through the nearby tunnels.

Faster and faster they moved. The pain pounded through Holly's nerves, but there was no time for her to slow down. She hobbled with one arm around Beth as fast as she was able.

The creature's screams suddenly grew louder as whatever it was entered the tunnel behind them.

"Juno?" Sarah called from behind.

"What?"

"The flare!" she said, pointing to Juno's hand where the flare fizzed. "It must be able to hear that!"

The group paused while Juno quickly hurled the flare behind them, back down the tunnel towards the bone dam.

"Come on," Beth said with urgency as she and Holly sped up again, followed by the rest.

Their headlamps and torches lit the way until they came to a fork in the tunnel. Veering left, they hobbled around the corner—only to come face-to-face with one of the creatures, a crawler.

It stood right in front of them, its jaw stretched impossibly wide, exposing its huge set of fangs. It hissed before shrieking at them.

Lunging forward, it reached for Holly, violently yanking her from Beth's grasp with ease.

"Run!" Rebecca screamed.

The sudden ferocity caused each of them to turn and run. There was no plan, no thought. They just needed to escape this thing as fast as possible.

In the chaos, Rebecca and Sam fled backwards and down the tunnel that forked off in the opposite direction. Sarah and Beth tried to follow, but soon lost sight of Rebecca and Sam through the winding tunnels and down a different path.

In the distance, a hideous shrieking mingled with Holly's desperate, garbled cries.

Juno, though, did not run away. She stood in front of the creature, pulled the pick from her belt, and screamed in defiance.

But the creature was already clawing at Holly, and it sank its long teeth into her neck. Her body writhed in panic as she tried to get away—but it was too late. The creature dug its claws into her sides and shook her violently, a predator disabling its prey. She flailed around like a rag doll as it tore more huge chunks out of her neck.

"Get away from her!" Juno screamed as she lunged at the crawler, the pick slicing through the air and cutting a large gash down the side of its pale face.

It staggered backwards and shrieked in pained anger, but its claws were still deep in Holly's convulsing torso, keeping a firm hold.

Sarah led as she and Beth rushed down a tunnel in a terrified panic.

Shrieks and screams echoed hauntingly behind them.

Beth suddenly lost her footing as she slipped on the moist rock beneath her boots. Stumbling to the floor, she landed with a painful thud and the wind was ripped from her lungs. Without the breath to call out to Sarah for help, Beth looked down the tunnel ahead, wheezing, but Sarah was already gone—completely unaware Beth was no longer behind her.

Sprinting in the opposite direction, but driven by the same fear, Sam and Rebecca continued down their chosen tunnel.

Pick in hand, Juno lunged again and again at the creature as it tried to drag Holly's body away. It lashed back at her with one claw, then bared its teeth as it shrieked in rage and ducked and writhed to avoid the pick.

Juno managed to grab Holly's injured leg by the ankle, but the crawler yanked her body away almost immediately, ripping her free from Juno's grasp.

The thing shrieked again, and Juno screamed back

louder. But before she could lunge with her pick again, a second crawler barrelled in from a side tunnel, barging into her and knocking her to the ground. Before she could get her bearings, the second creature was on top of her.

Without missing a beat, she let out a primal wail as she swung the pick upward and hacked away at the thing above her. Over and over, she repeatedly swung the pick into the beast's neck and head.

Holly's body was nearly out of sight, being dragged into the darkness. Her last drops of life ebbed away, and she weakly convulsed in the creature's grip.

Panting and exhausted, Rebecca and Sam emerged from their tunnel and into an unfamiliar chamber.

Sam turned back, confused. "Wait, where's the others?"

Staggering to her feet, Beth looked around, still winded. Disoriented, lost, and wheezing.

"Sarah?" she weakly spluttered.

Behind her, she heard the echo of Juno screaming bloody murder.

Despite multiple wounds from the pick, the crawler was still on top of Juno, screeching above her.

She smashed her pick once more into her attacker's side and pushed its bulk off. Kicking her way out, she scrambled to her feet, only to realise Holly was gone.

She took a few steps forward to give chase into the darkness, but before she could, the second crawler leapt onto her back, scraping at her face with its clawed hand as it lunged to bite at her neck.

Sarah stumbled blindly through the darkness as the light in her hand and on her helmet flailed.

She did not see where the ground dropped away in a steep slope.

Pitching forward, she tumbled over the precipice and downward, unable to stop the gravity pulling her.

Tumbling head over heels, she eventually landed ten feet below with a sickening thud onto cold, wet stone.

Juno, with the second crawler still latched onto her, fell backwards intentionally and slammed onto the unforgiving stone ground as hard as she could. The air left her lungs in a gasp, but she didn't stop. Instead, she thrust her head backwards with every ounce of force she could muster, bashing the back of her helmet straight into the creature's face. The sickening crack that sounded only fuelled her attack, and the creature's jaw shattered under her force. Blood, dark and viscous, sprayed out of its split mouth as she threw her head back once more. Cracking it again, with more of a wet squelch.

The crawler's talons twitched and it tried to defend itself, but it was too slow. Juno rolled over and drove her knee brutally into the centre of the creature's chest, the force compressing its ribs until they buckled inward with a hideous, splintering pop. The crawler screeched, its limbs flailing in desperation. But she didn't hear it—she didn't hear anything over the deafening roar of adrenaline.

Her eyes, blazing, locked onto the creature.

In one swift motion, she raised her pick and brought it down on its head. The pointed edge drove into its skull with a wet thunk and the bone split under the impact, cold metal sinking deep into its brain.

Quickly, she wrenched the pick free, only to slam it back down again. And again. And again. Each strike fuelled by her rage. With each successive hit, the creature's skull crunched farther inwards. Flesh gave way as bone cracked in, buckling like wet meat, revealing the pulpy, shattered remains of what was once its skull.

Juno kept swinging, harder and harder, the pick smashing through the already decimated head. The ground beneath it was a gory mess of blood, bone, and brain.

The creature's body twitched beneath her as if its nerves hadn't quite caught up to the fact that it was already very much dead—its head obliterated beyond recognition.

It took several seconds before the haze began to clear and she stopped swinging. Juno found herself atop her kill, staring down at its body, breathing raggedly. She shuddered.

Slowly, she stumbled to her feet, eyes wide and in deep shock. Trying to centre herself, she concentrated on managing her breathing. As she did, she listened.

Above the silence, she could only hear the pulse in her ears.

Then, suddenly, a scraping movement came from behind her.

She whirled as she let out a vicious roar, pick in hand, swinging at her attacker.

The silence suddenly returned.

Juno's rage gave way to a stupefied horror. Her mouth fell open in confusion.

Standing before her was Beth, looking at her with a blank expression.

Both stared at each other, unable to fathom what had just happened, until Beth collapsed to her knees, dragging Juno down with her.

The pick was firmly embedded in Beth's neck.

In shock, Juno could not let go of the handle.

Beth could only gasp as she reached out to Juno, her silent plea for help etched in every desperate and trembling motion. Her fingers found the edge of Juno's collar, clutching at the necklace around her neck. Juno pulled back sharply in a panic, and the chain snapped under the tension, leaving it and the attached pendant caught in Beth's grasp.

Only as Beth slumped to the side did the pick release from her neck. A large jet of dark arterial blood sprayed out and over Juno.

Beth's mouth jittered open and closed as she tried to speak, tried to beg for help. Her guttural gargles were eclipsed by multiple crawlers in the distance. Their roars grew louder down the tunnels as they neared.

Getting to her feet, Juno stared speechlessly down at Beth, and then down the tunnel where the shrieks were emanating from.

Beth could only look up incredulously, knowing what Juno was about to do.

Leave her.

Juno slowly backed away.

"Please," Beth managed to say in a weak gurgle. With the pendant still caught between her fingers, she reached up to her neck, trying to stifle her gushing blood. "Juno." What was left of her voice was filled with panic. "Please, don't leave me."

"I can't help you," Juno whispered, more to herself than Beth, then turned and fled from the oncoming shrieks.

Beth continued to grasp weakly at her neck. Her hands were soaked in her own blood and she desperately tried to stop the inevitable.

Rebecca and Sam stood in a cavern, waiting, listening. Terrified.

"What happened to them?" Sam asked quietly.

"We have to go back," Rebecca said, trying to force herself into not simply running away. "We can't just leave them, right?"

Before they could discuss it further, a shriek pierced the darkness, approaching them.

Rebecca grabbed Sam by the arm and dragged her away in the opposite direction. "Come on!"

Chapter 10

THE HUNTED

The camcorder, still recording, lay on its side at the bottom of the pitch-black drop.

Through its infrared viewfinder, Sarah's body could be seen lying unconscious on the stone floor. A trickle of blood dripped down her forehead from underneath her helmet, and the lamp affixed to it was cracked and broken. Her eyelids flittered as her face twitched, deep in a dream.

"Happy birthday!" Sarah said softly.

Her voice was filled with love, and she placed the birthday cake in front of Jessica. The five candles flickered brightly in the dim living room, casting a soft glow on her daughter's innocent face.

Standing on the other side of Jessica's chair, Paul smiled lovingly at Sarah and then to Jessica.

Everything at first seemed perfect. The curtains were drawn tightly, the air warm, yet it was also sticky with the stench of the rotten food. The kitchen radio played the discordant strains of a nightmarish version of "Happy Birthday".

Sarah and Paul glanced at each other.

"I love you, darling," Sarah said with a loving smile.

He smiled back and opened his mouth to speak.

But instead of words, a loud, monstrous shriek came out.

Sarah's eyes sprang open. She drew in a deep breath. Her heart raced as she realised where she was and what had happened.

With her headlamp broken and her torch no longer in her hand, the only visible thing in this chamber was the glow that emanated from the camcorder. Its power light. Everything else was masked in a black shroud of darkness, and all she knew was that she was lying on stone and that the camcorder was within arm's reach.

She scrambled forward and her head pounded, but it was nothing she could concern herself with.

Now, she had only one thought: to survive.

Grabbing the camcorder, she spun it around and opened the viewfinder. Its infrared night mode was the only vision she had.

Her breaths grew shallow and quick. As panic flooded through her senses, she spun the camera around the room. Desperate to find an exit. Desperate to see anything that could help.

A smell caught in her throat, a meaty, metallic, horrifically feculent smell. A stench so strong she could almost taste it. She had to concentrate to get past it.

Focusing on the screen, she noticed that something was half-buried among the loose soil and jagged debris a few feet ahead—an old, rusted oil lamp. Its glass was fractured, and its brass casing bent inward. She squinted, noticing faint, peeling letters barely legible through the rust. She could just make out a name. Taylor.

Moving over to it, she noticed a thick black liquid pooling out of it from one side. She dipped her finger in the liquid and brought it to her nose. Oil. The smell was strong and unmistakable. Wiping the remnants on her trousers, she remembered she had a lighter in her pocket and that maybe she could make a torch—but then she saw it.

Her trembling fingers adjusted the camcorder's focus as it slipped away from the broken lamp and drew in sharp on the jagged rocks behind it. Her breath stuttered. They were not rocks.

At the dam they had chanced upon earlier, the bones were disturbing enough, but they were clearly from wild animals—horned skulls, antlers, canine jaws. Gruesome, yes, but here before her now, this was different.

These were unmistakably human.

Her hands shook as the camera focused on the scattered bones. Skulls—so many skulls—were strewn haphazardly among the huge piles of other old human remains. No flesh, no sinew. Some were still eerily intact, with jaws still attached and vacant eye sockets that stared directly at her. Other remains had been smashed in, their tops caved with such force it was clear the damage to them was deliberate. Spines curled beside shattered ribcages, some split wide open, with the ribs snapped outward as if opened to find a prize inside.

There were not only old human remains here with her. Next, the camera fell upon what was left of dozens of animals. She stared at the viewfinder in horror while she panned the camcorder over what resembled an ancient underground abattoir. As she panned, the remains grew more recent. Some animals lay in a newer, slaughtered state. Their flesh still rotted as blood matted in their decaying fur.

A giant elk with its antlers snapped off stared blankly at her with carved-out eyes, its stomach torn open and emptied of all its insides. Other deer lay in pieces, with flesh and fur peeled off parts of their bones.

It was from these newer remains that the smell emanated.

With her jaw chattering and hands trembling, Sarah turned the camera away from the disgusting tableau, hoping to find a way out through another part of this nightmarish room.

Behind her, beyond the top of the steep incline where she had fallen, a monstrous growl made Sarah freeze. Quickly and as silently as possible, she closed the viewfinder on the camcorder and covered its LEDs with her hand, casting herself into total darkness.

Far above, a beam of dull light appeared and flitted around.

Sarah's heart leapt. It has to be one of my friends, she thought.

But then the light spiralled downward in a fast free-fall.

Scrambling out of the way, Sarah nearly avoided the large object that smashed down into the rock before her with a wet thud and a crack.

The light she had seen tumbling from above now lay on the ground. A snap light illuminated the immediate area, casting an eerie glow over what it was attached to. Sarah recoiled as the clawed, eyeless face of Holly stared back at her. Her body was gouged, battered, and blood-soaked.

Juno could no longer hold the small amount of food left in her stomach. Staggering against the nearest wall, she vomited. The bile stung her throat as it spewed up and out.

Behind her, shrieks and roars of many creatures echoed down the tunnel. A cacophony of primal ferocity forced her to keep moving. Wiping her mouth on her sleeve, she moved on. She had no time to gather her thoughts, no time to worry that her stomach may have more to reject.

"Up there!" Rebecca said in an urgent hush, pointing to a ledge high up along the tunnel wall. "Hurry," she urged Sam. The rush of crawlers grew louder and closer behind them.

Wasting no time, they both jumped up to the ledge and then pulled themselves onto it. As Sam swung her leg over the side, the activated snap lights slipped from her grasp and clattered down to the dirt floor below. Their blue glow cast a cold hue over the lower part of the tunnel.

Sam moved her leg back over to retrieve them, but Rebecca grabbed her by the shoulder.

"Leave them!" Rebecca whispered. She switched off her headlamp and torch, then crawled farther onto the ledge.

Sam followed quickly, turning her lights off and crawling beside her sister. Both lay down, pushing themselves into the darkness of the crevice as tightly as they could, hoping the monsters would rush by and miss them.

Sarah, finding the strength, slowly opened the camcorder's viewfinder again. The infrared displayed Holly's mutilated corpse in much more grotesque clarity.

Sarah was about to gasp at the sight, but a new noise from the top of the slope caused her to grab her mouth. Holding in any noise as tight as she could.

She watched through the camcorder's viewfinder as several crawlers emerged from up top then climbed down into the cavern, only a few feet in front of her.

As they sniffed the air, the creatures approached Holly's body, crawling on all fours towards her. Their heads twitched from left to right as they cautiously surrounded her corpse.

The largest one, with a fresh wound down its face, held up its clawed hand and brought it down with force into Holly's belly. Its terrifying talons tore through her jacket and skin with ease before ripping outward and spilling her intestines onto the stony floor.

Closing her eyes, Sarah held back the gagging that threatened to escape her throat. She had to be quiet.

Each of the crawlers tore portions of flesh from Holly. They ate whatever meat they could rip, slurping and smacking their teeth as they feasted on her torn remains.

Sarah squeezed her eyes even tighter, as if doing so would also shut out the sickening sounds.

The largest wounded crawler, halfway through chewing on a length of dripping colon, suddenly stopped. As it did, it let its food fall from its sharp mouth and slop to its feet.

The creature tilted its head to the side.

Something was there that shouldn't have been.

Sarah kept her eyes shut, reeling from the sounds that had filled the air moments before. The sickening crunch of tearing flesh and the wet, brutal ripping all ceased, replaced by a gut-churning silence so sudden it seemed to suck the air from around her.

No more scraping claws. No shrieks. Nothing.

It was as though everything had simply vanished.

Her heart pounded in her ears. Against every instinct screaming inside her, she forced her eyes open to glance down to the viewfinder. She dreaded having to see Holly's deathly expression again, especially in its current condition.

She froze.

Inches from her face, it was there. The creature.

Its grotesque, angular face was now so close to her own. With its blotchy skin caked in filth, its mouth lolling open, it sniffed the air around her. As it did, its tongue peeked out between its sharp fangs and flicked at the air, as if to taste what it could smell.

Sarah held her breath. She fought against everything in her mind to ensure she stayed silent.

The creature's closed eyes then snapped open—wide,

unblinking, revealing two sickly yellow orbs that glinted in the glowing hue of the viewfinder.

These few moments stretched on, agonising and surreal.

The crawler's slitted nose twitched closer, its chest rising slowly as it took in a deep lungful.

But then, as the crawlers behind it resumed their meal, the creature's attention was pulled back to them. With an angry shriek, it scurried back over, sank its claws into Holly's face, and dragged her corpse nearer to it. Claiming it.

The other crawlers shied away as they lowered their heads in reverence to what had to be an alpha beast.

Sarah shut her eyes again as the monstrous meal continued. She wondered why she hadn't been seen. Is it blind? It must have smelled me, she thought. From her fall into this terrible room, she had been covered in filth and that the terrible stench of rot was all over her, masking her natural odour.

Saving her.

Rebecca and Sam both felt the cold stone pressing against their faces where they lay hidden on the narrow ledge, their hearts pounding. They huddled close in the darkness, terrified to make the slightest sound.

Sam felt a rush of anxiety flood through her. She pictured the glowing blue snap lights scattered below on the tunnel floor—small beacons that might as well have been flashing arrows pointing directly at their hiding place.

A deep, guttural exhalation came as a crawler entered from the adjacent chamber. Its heavy, uneven breathing filled the silence as it stepped forward. Its head jerked erratically from side to side, twitching, listening for any sign of movement. Hunting. Slowly, its feet left the floor as it crawled up the wall.

Sam's chest tightened. She couldn't suppress the quiet gasp that escaped her lips. Rebecca's instincts kicked in immediately and she leaned over and pressed her hand firmly to her sister's mouth.

For a short time, the creature stopped. So much so that Rebecca almost moved to peer over the ledge to check the coast was clear, but a scraping against the rock above them made her pull Sam in even tighter. In that instant, both realised that the creature was now scaling the wall above them, edging closer and closer.

The creature sniffed the air as it crawled less than a foot above them. Its tongue licked at the air, and it lowered a gaunt, clammy, clawed hand onto the ledge, millimetres away from Sam's face.

As it moved off the wall, it crouched on the ledge so close that they could smell its rotten stink. The glow from the snap lights on the floor below cast this creature in a pale blue hue, illuminating the hundreds of healed scars all over its pockmarked, pallid skin.

They remained as still and silent as they could while the creature sat on its haunches, its head twitching as it listened intently.

After a few tense beats, the creature climbed off the ledge and carried on with its search down the next tunnel.

Cautiously, Rebecca removed her hand from Sam's mouth.

"It couldn't see us," Sam whispered, stating the obvious.

Rebecca shrugged as best she could, trying to figure out when they would be able to move.

After minutes ticked by and the silence remained, the coast seemed to be as clear as it could be.

A sharp bleeping suddenly emitted from Sam's watch. In the silence, this beeping was so loud it was almost deafening.

Down in the tunnel, the crawler reeled and it threw back its head into a roar.

"No," Sam whimpered. She struggled with the strap of the watch. When it came loose, she immediately threw it from the ledge and as far down the tunnel as she could aim.

Almost instantly, a crawler appeared from the opposite tunnel and let out a wail as it chased the beeping.

Sam and Rebecca lay there, praying for a miracle.

Along a narrow, dank tunnel, Juno held up a green snap light in front of her. Its glow cast long, dark shadows off the jagged rocks that stuck out from the walls, making them seem so much larger than they were. Every deliberate step she took was painfully slow yet silent.

The pick, still wet with blood, was firmly gripped in her other hand, ready to strike if needed.

She paused every few steps, her body tense and alert, as she strained to hear anything other than the monotonous dripping of water. Her heart thudded, but she forced herself to remain calm, to not focus on what had happened. She had friends to find, people lost somewhere in this labyrinth, and she couldn't afford to make any more mistakes.

Reaching a junction where several tunnels split off in various directions, Juno's gaze locked onto something on the stone wall to her right: a crude arrow hastily scrawled and barely visible beneath layers of grime and moss. An arrow that pointed down one of the tunnels.

She glanced around her in every direction, holding the snap light in front of her as her eyes darted between the burrows. She listened again to the silence. Every muscle in her body tensed.

Then she heard it: a soft, almost imperceptible sound. The faint, haunting whistle of a breeze. Subtle and barely there, but unmistakable.

A breeze that meant only one thing.

A way out.

Sarah, still trapped witnessing this monster's butchery, squeezed her eyes shut, but had no other choice than to listen to her friend's corpse being ripped apart and consumed.

The few times she dared to open her eyes to see if they had finished, she witnessed such horrors, drenched in the glow of the snap light, that they would be forever burnt into her memory.

From elsewhere, the clatter of a falling rock carried through the tunnels and into the cavern.

Then came a voice.

"Sarah?" the voice cried out, carrying faintly through the air.

The creatures immediately stopped their meal and, in

one sudden burst, darted up the drop and out of the cavern in pursuit.

Even though it had been barely audible, Sarah knew whose voice it was. Juno's.

Through the viewfinder, Holly's remains were almost impossible to recognise. Her face had been gnawed off, leaving only a tuft or two of matted hair in its place. Her whole body had been lacerated and gored repeatedly, almost completely stripped of all meat and fat from the bones.

"Shit," Juno cursed as she arrived at yet another junction between two tunnels.

Again, she listened. Nothing.

Holding the pick ready, she steeled herself and summoned the bravery to call out again. "Sarah?" she said loudly. "Rebecca? Sam? Can anyone hear me?" She gripped the pick defensively, expecting something to jump out, then peered down each tunnel, waiting, listening. "Where are you?"

Rebecca and Sam, still on the ledge, huddled closer when they heard the voice come from farther down one of the tunnels.

"It's Juno," Sam whispered. "What's she doing?"

Rebecca shook her head. "The noise she's making, she'll bring every one of those things down on her head."

"As long as it's not on mine."

"Well, we can't stay here forever," Rebecca said. "That thing must have moved on by now."

*

"I'm sorry," Sarah said mournfully as she stared at Holly's fractured, ruined body. Peering down at what was left of her leg, Sarah reached and pulled the pick handle that had been used as a splint.

Through Holly's snapped bone and mushy flesh, it came out easily. The straps that once were tightly tied on her calf hung loose and torn over the stripped and broken bone.

Holding her breath to steel her nerves, Sarah quickly lifted Holly's upper body into a seated position. She removed the stripped remnants of her jacket as fast as she could, then wrapped the partially damp material around one end of the pick handle.

Scrambling over to the miner's lamp, she picked it up and moved back over to the snap light.

"Please, please, please, please." In a panic, she broke the lid off the miner's lamp, then tipped it upside down over the now-tied jacket. As a slick of old, viscous oil dripped out over the edge of the lamp, she could not help but smile through her welling tears. The oil poured over the jacket, mixing with the blood and fabric.

Then she quickly produced a lighter. One flick of the flint later, the oil on the jacket tied to the end of the pick handle ignited, catching fire with ease.

The killing room around her was illuminated by the bright orange glow of her makeshift torch.

After studying the steep slope she had previously fallen down, it became clear she would not be able to climb up there again. Instead, she moved deeper across the expansive lair, treading between the detritus of death, hoping to find another exit. As she did, the tears finally spilled down her cheeks as the gravity of what was happening hit her hard.

But she had to push through.

Chapter 11

HOPE AND HORROR

Another arrow appeared under the dim glow of Juno's snap light, crudely scrawled onto the damp stone wall of the tunnel. She moved the light over it and pressed on with a determined step. She had to keep moving, had to believe that she was getting closer to saving her and everyone else.

Every—

Beth. Holly.

No.

She forged on ahead up the twisted rocky path, but another junction soon opened before her. Two very narrow and low tunnels jutted off in opposite directions.

Before choosing which way to go, she turned and shouted, "Rebecca? Sam? Sarah?"

A high-pitched, unnatural shriek split the air, shattering the stillness like glass.

A cold rush of adrenaline washed through her veins. On instinct, Juno spun on her heel, raising her pick defensively, eyes wide and breathing shallow. Her gaze shot around the tunnel and she tried to determine which direction the noise had come from.

Rebecca and Sam heard the shriek, too. Their hearts pounded as they instinctively pressed themselves against the rough, damp wall. This monstrous cry was closer to them than it had been to Juno. Much closer.

Rebecca's eyes fixed on the darkened corner ahead. A wave of renewed dread washed over her. The creature felt so close now, like the source of that noise lurked just ahead, directly in their path. They had to move.

"Don't," Sam said nervously when Rebecca stepped forward, her voice barely more than a whisper as she pleaded.

But Rebecca stepped forward cautiously. Every muscle in her body was taut, and cold beads of sweat trickled down her brow. She passed the darkness in front of them and breathed a sigh of relief when no monster was hidden within it.

In the next tunnel they arrived at a corner, and Rebecca paused while she summoned every ounce of resolve. Slowly, she leaned around the turn, expecting the worst in the darkness.

But her headlamp only illuminated an empty passage.

Rebecca exhaled a shaky breath she hadn't realised she was holding.

"It's clear," she whispered.

Sam glanced behind them, her eyes darting back into the blackness. Her headlamp split the shadow. She, too, saw nothing. No movement, no sound.

The tension eased and they both continued forward,

cautiously stepping around the turn into the next stretch.

Before they could take another step, a claw shot down from the ceiling, colliding with Rebecca's shoulder and slashing her skin open. As she screamed, she pulled herself back and raised her pick.

Her lamp shone over a crawler hanging from the ceiling. Its clawed feet grappled to the rock above, holding its weight as it shrieked at them.

Rebecca's pick glided through the air but missed the target. The crawler shrieked again and opened its blank yellow eyes.

"Get back," Rebecca shouted to Sam as she backed away.

Both held their picks up at the monster, ready to strike.

But the crawler was not threatened or deterred by them or their weapons. It crawled across the ceiling, matching their pace as they backed away. It clicked and gurgled, and its blind eyes remained open.

Rebecca swiped the pick in the air again. She knew she was out of reach but hoped her movement would scare it off. A show of strength and threat that some creatures would normally bolt at. Not this one.

While their attention was stuck firmly on the advancing creature, the tunnel behind them came to another junction and their backs hit a stone wall. The two tunnels snaked backwards, and if they tried to run now, the crawler would catch them with its claws.

"Sam," Rebecca said through gritted teeth. "When I say, run to the left, got it? I'll hold it back."

"I won't go without you," Sam cried out.

"Just do it on three," she said, and she gripped her pick tightly. "One... Two... Now."

Sam ducked low and sprinted into the left-hand tunnel just as Rebecca let out a fierce yell and swung the pick. The blow narrowly missed the hanging crawler's face, forcing it to recoil instinctively.

Rebecca wasted no time, aiming another strike at the creature's exposed head. But before the pick could connect, the crawler lashed out. One taloned hand batted the weapon from her grasp, sending it clattering to the ground. Its other claw shot forward, closing around her throat in a vicelike grip.

It crawled off the ceiling to the floor and squeezed her tighter in its cold, rough palm. With extreme ease, it lifted her up as if she weighed nothing, then slammed her against the uneven wall of the tunnel.

Moving its face closer to hers, it growled.

But then Rebecca heard a yelp from the tunnel behind her.

Sam.

Her world sank. Her throat closed.

The crawler's jaws opened and opened and opened. Its full set of sharp fangs was displayed in its impossibly huge maw.

It lunged closer, ready to take a bite, but before its mouth could envelop her head, another pick came whooshing out of the darkness. It collided with the back of the creature, slicing into its shoulders with a squelch.

The growls from the creature turned into an intensely high wheeze, and its entire head began to tremble. Its hungry mouth lolled open in loose shock. Its blind eyes went as wide as they could go.

Its grip around Rebecca's throat loosened, and then its claws fell away.

Buckling backwards, it reached its arms behind to try and grab the pick protruding from its back.

Rebecca stared in grateful shock at Juno standing there, flanked by Sam.

As the creature grunted, staggering backwards, Rebecca's happiness turned to sudden fury and she scrambled to the floor to get her pick. Then she slammed the metal into the downed crawler's chest.

While it reeled, Juno yanked her pick from the creature's back then attacked it again, as did Rebecca. Both ferociously swung at the beast. Their blades stabbed and pierced and sliced.

The cries from the creature pitched even higher, like desperate pleas for help, as they hacked and hacked and hacked.

Once its head hit the dirt, Sam ran forward and stomped on its throat with all her weight, cutting off any noise in a pained gargle as its windpipe crushed inward.

In the middle of a large chamber, with her flaming torch in hand, Sarah stopped as she heard the creature's distant, tortured cries.

She paused.

Waiting.

Listening.

*

Holding a rock above her, Juno grunted then slammed it down onto the creature's head.

It tried to howl in terror through its damaged throat, but the rock slammed into its face. A torrent of blood burst outward, silencing it immediately.

The creature's body trembled, its head broken under the rock, and the three women stood back.

Sarah moved through the low-hanging vaults at the back of the chamber. She trod as silently as she could, but small cracks could be heard underfoot, threatening to alert the creatures. She glanced around nervously.

Juno and Rebecca shared a tight embrace while Sam stared at the dead creature.

"We heard you calling. What happened?" Rebecca asked, careful not to talk too loudly.

"Have you seen the others?" Sam asked.

Juno tried to smile to ease the news. But there was nothing she could say to soften what she had to tell them. "Holly's dead," she said with a whimper.

Sam's expression fell into shock.

"Beth—"

Juno just shook her head, unable to speak the words.

The three fell silent, not one able to process what was happening.

"They look—" Sam said, trying to control her emotions as she focused on the creature. "They look almost human."

"Come on," Rebecca said as she gripped her pick. "I don't want to stand around and wait for more of those things to come out."

"Wait! Sam," Juno said, "you got a good look at it. Can you tell anything about it?"

"What would she know?" Rebecca asked incredulously.

"She's almost a doctor, right?" Juno replied. "She knows biology, and... I don't know."

"She's not a vet, Juno!"

"Yeah, but like she said, it looks almost human." She turned to Sam. "Right?"

"Right," Sam replied, unconvinced. She looked at her sister, then down at the dead creature. "I think it's blind. And from what we've seen, it probably uses sound and smell to... see with. To hunt with, like..." She paused. "...like a bat or something? So, it's got all it needs to live down here."

"Why does anything live down here?" Rebecca asked.

"People lived in these caves, right?" Juno said. "The ones who were on those cave paintings. Then, I guess these things..."

"You think these things ate the cavemen or something?"

"Or are they the cavemen?" Sam said.

Juno and Rebecca turned to her with quizzical expressions.

"What if, back then," Sam continued, "there were cavemen or whatever? Maybe some went outside to live, maybe some stayed in the caves. Maybe we evolved up there, and they evolved... down here?"

"That's a lot of maybes." Rebecca shrugged.

"Well, we saw all those animal bones, right?" Juno said.

"And?" Rebecca asked.

"And they gotta eat. They have to access the surface to hunt, right? To get those animals." Juno slowly smiled. "They must've brought their food down here to eat it. That was the bones."

"So, there has to be another exit?!" Sam smiled in relief.

Juno nodded. "If we can stay quiet enough and evade these fuckers... I think I know how we can get out. Back there." She tipped her head in the direction she had come from.

"You think you know?" Rebecca asked.

"Those miners that must have come down here. I think they marked their route so they could find their way back out... I've found loads of arrows drawn on walls. We just gotta follow them."

"What are we waiting for?" Sam asked.

"Sarah," Juno replied in a grim tone. "We have to find Sarah."

Sweeping the torch back and forth, Sarah stepped farther into the far reaches of the expansive lair. She grew numb to the sea of dead animal bodies that surrounded her. Ancient and new, they were piled haphazardly around, leaving little room to walk without having to clamber over them.

Her foot suddenly slipped backwards after it landed on something wet. Tipping forward, her hand shot out to brace her fall. She hit the floor hard and she let out a pained moan, dropping the torch from her hands and sensing a warm moisture below.

After a few seconds, she tried to get her bearings. Reaching for the torch, she noticed her palm dripped with blood. Warm blood.

She clambered to her feet and moved her torch in front of her to see where the blood had come from.

Behind her, the remains of a recently butchered deer lay splayed open. From underneath it, a leg stuck out. A human leg. A leg that had chunks of flesh stripped away from the bone. The muscles left on it had been ripped by sharp teeth and claws. The blood that oozed from it pooled on the ground beneath her.

The leg still wore a boot. A familiar boot.

"Oh god," she whispered. "No!"

Frantically, Sarah dropped her torch and yanked the remnants of the deer off the body. It lay there, face down.

"Please, no, Beth!" Sarah screamed. She turned the body over. She whimpered when she saw her friend's face and the bloody wound in her neck.

"Beth," Sarah repeated, overcome with intense grief. Tears fell down her cheeks.

Beth's eyes snapped open and her hand shot up to grab Sarah by the arm.

"Run," she said with a laboured wheeze.

Sarah jolted with shock as her grief flipped to relief. "I'm going to get you out of here, okay?"

Grasping for strength, Beth's words came out guttural and rough. "I can't move. I can't—" She forced the words out, but they were growing fainter. "I can't feel... anything."

"Beth," Sarah said weakly.

"Even when those... things... started... eating," she said, and then she began to cough. Blood spilled out over her lips.

"I heard Juno earlier," Sarah said, speaking with as much reassured strength as possible. Trying to convince Beth all was not lost. "She's alive. She must be nearby. I'm going to go and find her, and we're going to get you out. We'll find Rebecca and Sam—"

"Stay away from Juno," Beth rasped, angry. "She did this to me." She took a long, painful breath. "She attacked me... then left me... to them."

"No, that can't be, Beth," Sarah pleaded.

"Listen to me," Beth hissed, using all the strength she had left. She raised her head, and blood from her neck wound started to flow again. "You can't trust her. She doesn't care about us. She... killed... me."

"She's our friend!" Sarah protested. "She's—"

"She's a lying cunt. Always has been." Before Sarah could reply, she continued. "She was fucking him."

"W-What?"

"Paul. She was fucking him behind your back."

Sarah's words fell away. She stared at Beth's furious expression. She knew Beth would never lie to her, and she knew that Juno was her friend. She knew... What did she know?

Her mind whirled with images of her past. The furtive glances between her husband and Juno that Sarah had dismissed as friendliness. The times Paul had mentioned her, asked about her. No... They couldn't have been...

"Juno wouldn't do that to me," she muttered.

Beth coughed as blood spluttered out, snapping Sarah

out of her thoughts. "I-I'm sorry," Beth gurgled and held up her other hand.

Hanging from her bloodied and bruised fingers was Juno's necklace.

Taking it, Sarah stared down at the pendant on the chain. She turned it over in her hand and saw an engraving soaked in Beth's blood. Wiping it with her thumb, she revealed three words: Love Each Day.

In the distance, a crawler shrieked. A brief beat, and then it shrieked again, nearer.

"Sarah, please," Beth pleaded. "Don't leave me to them."

"What?" Sarah asked, unable to focus through her turmoil.

"End it, please," Beth wheezed. "Don't let them..."

Sarah stared back. Her world had been crushed again. More stolen from her than simply her family's life. It was her love now stolen, too. Her mind twisted upside down.

Gripping the pendant tight, she stared at Beth as more shrieks rang out from the tunnels and into the lair.

"Please..."

Then something changed in her.

A chill slipped over Sarah. Like an ice blanket that covered her thoughts, blocking out everything trying to torment her. Her worried expression fell.

"I love you," Beth gurgled. "Please..."

The tears streaking Sarah's cheeks stopped falling. She smiled at Beth as kindly as she could.

"Please," Beth pleaded.

Another shriek.

"Close your eyes," Sarah whispered.

Chapter 12
ATTACK

The flame from Sarah's torch cast flickering shadows over her face. Its yellow-and-orange hue danced across her steeled expression. With her eyes closed, a numbness had begun to consume her. She could feel her mind closing in, protecting her from breaking apart.

She did not see the mental images of her beloved Beth as the rock mercifully crushed the life from her. She did not see Holly's decimated body ripped asunder by those creatures. She saw only one thing when she closed her eyes.

"Happy birthday!" she said softly.

With her eyes still closed, she could see Jessica smiling at her. The five candles on her cake lit up the dim room.

"I love you, Jessie-bear."

A growl nearby caused Sarah to open her eyes. She swung the torch around to look behind her. Perched on top of a bone pile was a lone crawler on its haunches, facing her.

Sarah gritted her teeth as the fear grew inside. Then she bolted in the opposite direction, towards a wide fissure on the far side of the room. Clambering over piles of animal carcasses as she went, she heard another noise from the creature.

A battle cry.

But, glancing over her shoulder, she saw that the creature was still there, perched on the bone pile.

Why doesn't it follow? she thought in a panic. Is it the torch? Is it afraid of fire?

Her boots crushed fragments of bones beneath her.

Another cry sounded.

She sped up.

Just this final stretch of rock to run across before—

The ground beneath her began to shift as her footing gave way, plunging her headfirst into a large pool. The flaming torch launched forward from her grasp and hit the far wall, where it landed in the dirt.

At this end of the cavern, the floor sank to its lowest point. Over many years, it must've become a drainage pool—a cesspit of unspeakable filth that had collected all the blood, gore, and foul liquid that slimed down the rocks to make this swamp—where all the dripping waste had gathered and congealed into a thick, sludgy mire. Decades of slaughter, animals and humans, ripped apart and opened wide, with every drippable liquid that had seeped down the incline now ended up here. Gallons upon gallons of blood, bile, and excrement mixed with liquefying flesh and sinew without a way for it to drain. A sickening stew of death.

A layer of rock-looking muck had crusted its surface and hid the reality of what lay beneath—until Sarah's boot broke through. As Sarah fell in, it released a stench that had been trapped from years of stagnation. Her body splashed into the muck and the air exploded with a putrid, acrid tang of decomposition and waste.

Sarah sank through the filth, falling a few feet beneath the surface.

A few seconds passed as the muck sloshed around, before Sarah resurfaced and gasped for air. Her eyes opened wide and she yelled in fury.

All traces of her beauty and humanity were coated in the terrible sludge.

From this grotesque baptism, Sarah screamed again—as terrifying as any of the crawler's shrieks and roars. She turned to face the crawler, expecting to see it still hunched on the bone pile. But the light from her downed flame did not illuminate that part of the cave. It only had enough strength to send its dull orange glow over the meaty swamp.

Turning back to the fissure in the wall, Sarah did not have a chance to walk forward before the crawler burst out of the bloody pool in front of her. Launching upward with a wail, its clawed hands came down and collided with her shoulders, pushing them both back down into the viscera.

As quickly as they sank, the two reemerged, grappling ferociously at each other.

Gripping both hands around the crawler's throat, Sarah could feel the terrifying coldness of its skin. Not a trace of warmth remained under her touch. The beast was as cold as any of the corpses.

In return, the creature reached out and grabbed her throat, but this beast was significantly stronger, its hands much tougher. Its claws were a natural weapon, whereas she had none.

With ease, the crawler forced Sarah's head back down into the gore, holding her under as it howled victoriously.

Her hands around its neck fell away, unable to keep a grip.

She struggled to breathe in the mire, but her hands tracked through the filth, looking for something, anything, that could help her.

The crawler pulled her back up by the throat before it thrust her back down under again. Without time to gasp for air, as she sank back under, the blood and muck flowed into her gaping mouth.

Her hands fell back down and they brushed against something at the bottom of the pool. Something solid.

She gripped it with her right hand when she was dragged upward a second time. The solid object—a large rib from a deer—snapped off the ribcage beneath the gore. Holding it like a dagger, as soon as her hand left the liquid, Sarah jabbed the rib straight at the crawler's face, piercing its blind eye.

The creature wailed and released its grip on her. It staggered back through the waste, the rib sticking out of its eye socket.

Spitting out the gore from her mouth, Sarah quickly rushed at the creature and slammed the end of the bone with her hand, driving it deeper into its socket and through its brain, sending it crashing backwards into the muck.

Jumping on top of its submerged body, she then held

the beast down. She pushed her full weight down upon it, and the little life it had left soon disappeared.

Breathing heavily and still tasting the foulness in the back of her throat, Sarah glanced around for more creatures possibly lying in wait.

She fought her way through the thick muck, wading over countless horrors below. Reaching the far side, she pulled herself up onto the ridge and out of the bile. Sarah crawled onto the dirt beside her still-flaming torch, where she collapsed in a heap, face down. Gasping for air.

Coated from head to foot in gore, she had little energy to even wipe her face, so she just lay there. Trying to get her breath. Trying to focus.

A sudden scraping behind her caused Sarah to instinctively hold her breath and fall completely still.

Heavy steps came from inside the fissure and along the ridge.

Facing away and out over the pool, Sarah could not see the crawler that had entered the lair. She could only see its large shadow projected across the death pool by the flaming torch beside her. In its silhouette, it appeared gargantuan.

The creature stopped on its haunches right next to her. It loudly sniffed the air. Sniffing for her. But all it could smell was the muck that covered her from the large pool.

She continued to hold her breath and shut her eyes as she concentrated on not moving.

Crawling forward, the beast's taloned hand came to rest directly on Sarah's coated head, and its other gripped the ridge edge overlooking the pool. It leaned forward, sniffing for her, listening for movement. As it did, its weight crushed down on her skull heavily.

The skin of its hand was so cold, so thick, it could not feel the warmth coming off her head. It grunted then crawled along the edge, still sniffing the air.

As its weight moved off her, Sarah opened her eyes in silent pain. She stared ahead, still not breathing, still deathly motionless. While she stared out, trying to swallow the pain, a large bone floated to the edge of the swamp in front of her.

Carefully, silently, and very slowly, as the creature crawled away, Sarah reached out and grabbed the bone from the filth. It was at least two feet long and very, very thick. A thigh bone from some large animal that had met its fate down in this dark hell.

The creature had its back to her now. She rose to her feet, holding the bone and stepping carefully to avoid alerting it.

Once she stood directly behind the crawler, she finally allowed herself to inhale loudly, not able to hold her breath anymore. With a weapon in hand, she was no longer afraid the monster would hear her.

Immediately, the creature's head turned back to her as it wailed loudly, just as the joint of the thigh bone crashed down on its skull.

It collapsed in a heap. The creature did not have a chance to stand up and fight before the bone came down on its head again.

Covered head to foot in the remnants of death, with

her eyes coloured by a savage rage, Sarah grabbed the torch with her other hand and stood over the creature's body.

In the distant tunnels, a cacophonous roar of creatures echoed.

Juno, Rebecca, and Sam stood in a wide tunnel. The shrieking chorus grew nearer.

"Shit," Sam muttered.

"That sounds like an army," Rebecca said, her voice tense.

Both of their faces mirrored the same defeated fear, like they were already resigned to the worst outcome.

Juno felt her stomach tighten as the noises sounded even closer. She pointed her pickaxe ahead. "Go," she said, putting her free hand on Rebecca's shoulder. "Follow the markings. Hurry."

"What about you?" Rebecca asked.

"I'll be right behind. Now, go before they get here!"

Rebecca and Sam vanished down the dark tunnel ahead, and Juno turned away with a mix of dread and determination. Her headlamp cast a pale, trembling light down the rough, uneven stone. Its feeble glow barely touched the jagged walls before being swallowed by the blackness beyond. Her breathing was shallow, and a cold sweat dripped down her back.

She took one step forward, and then the shrieks came again—louder, more savage, echoing off the walls like a rising tide.

Her pulse quickened and her throat tightened. She stood, fighting the instinct to run with Rebecca and Sam, knowing she couldn't leave without trying one last time to find Sarah.

"Sarah?!" her voice called out, trembling with desperation, hoping beyond hope for a response.

But the only answer was more relentless shrieking.

And then she saw them.

They emerged from the darkness of the tunnel like a nightmare—dozens upon dozens of them, crawling on all fours. On the floor, walls, and ceiling. Their grotesque bodies contorted as they skittered nearer, each howling as they clawed over the stone. The twisted shapes of their limbs moved unnaturally fast while their clawed hands and feet grappled against the stone with terrifying speed.

They moved as a pack. A coordinated swarm.

Their mouths stretched open wide and the shrieks filled the stale air.

Juno stepped back, seeing the unbeatable odds rushing towards her. She turned after Rebecca and Sam.

"Run!" she screamed, desperately racing down the tunnel. Behind her, the horrifying mass of limbs and teeth barrelled closer.

At a junction ahead, Juno saw Rebecca's and Sam's lights, their silhouettes lit up in the shadow.

Juno, still determined not to leave her friend behind, called out as she ran. "Sarah?"

Rebecca's face twisted in anguish. "She's dead, Juno! We can't wait for her!"

Her words hit like a physical blow, the finality of it cutting through her denial. She knew Rebecca was right.

“Come on!” Sam shouted back. She bolted ahead, her figure quickly disappearing into the shadows of the left-hand tunnel.

“Sam, wait!” Rebecca called after her.

The tunnels ahead seemed endless, winding, twisting in every direction. It was a disorienting maze of stone and shadow, but they ran as fast as they could.

Juno could hear the crawlers behind her. Their guttural snarls and the relentless scrape of claws against rock grew louder with every second.

Sam led the way. Her movements were quick, driven by a purely terrified survival instinct. Rebecca, just behind her, tried to keep up but felt the constant need to glance over her shoulder to Juno.

And Juno, who was a dozen paces behind, did not risk any backwards glance. She could sense what was there. She could hear them screaming for blood. The shrieks and scrapes of the crawlers were relentless.

The tunnel narrowed but they hurtled forward, barely able to keep their footing on the rocky ground. The walls began to close in around them, but there was no time to think and plan—only to run.

Every turn down a tunnel that had been marked with an arrow was a gamble. An unknown path that could lead them either deeper into danger or grant them freedom. They didn’t have the luxury of pondering whether the arrows were really a saviour or their damnation. They simply prayed as they ran.

Suddenly, the ground beneath them slanted as the tunnel

dipped into a steep slope. Sam stumbled but caught herself as her momentum carried her forward. Rebecca wasn't so lucky: she tripped, her hands scraping against the rough stone as she tried to steady herself. Hearing her sister's yelp, Sam turned back, grabbed Rebecca's arm, and pulled her up to her feet. Rebecca limped on, her ankle twisted.

As they reached the next tunnel, Sam—grabbing tight to Rebecca's arm as she hobbled along—followed an arrow caught in the dull glow from her headlamp.

The advancing howls behind them had not yet caught up.

If Juno had paused to think about it, she would have wondered why. Why these terrifying beasts had not caught them by now, since they were much faster and in much greater numbers. They knew these tunnels. *Are they playing with us?* But she had no time to ponder this, only time to run.

Ahead of them, the tunnel's ceiling dropped. So much so that all three had to drop onto all fours and crawl through the small fissure.

"Are you sure this is the way?" Sam asked.

"Move it!" Rebecca shouted behind her. "Faster."

Juno, at the back, gritted her teeth. She could only crawl as fast as the other two, and it was a lot slower than she would have liked to have gone.

Suddenly, a monstrous noise reverberated from behind them, so loud it caused Rebecca and Juno to pause and glance back, expecting to see the creatures advancing.

Sam scrambled frantically forward until the ground beneath her hands and knees abruptly disappeared, revealing a vast gorge with a sheer, steep drop. She gasped as she skidded to a halt at its very edge. Her hand pressed into the brittle stone, which crumbled under her weight. A cascade of loose rocks tumbled downward, falling deep into the black chasm. And after a short silence, the rocks splashed into a body of water.

The gap was reminiscent of the one they'd crossed earlier, but this time, there was no chance for careful planning or preparation. Hesitation wasn't an option. She had to act. Fast.

Sam's gaze swept the opposite side of the gorge and light caught on the ceiling above, where the cavern arched upward. She focused through her headlamp's glow along the surface until she spotted a long crack running to the other side. A crack just wide enough to grip.

Without pausing to think further or wait for the others, she reached for a piton from her belt. She jammed it into a crack in the wall beside her, pushing it in as securely as she could. The clang of metal against stone echoed in the gorge, but it barely registered.

She grabbed a spool of rope from her belt and tied one end to the piton. Her eyes darted back to the tunnel behind her—she saw Rebecca's light approaching.

Quickly, she jammed a cam in the ceiling and looped in the rope, then leaned forward. Her fingers found the jagged crack of the fissure. She clenched her hand, tested the grip, and let her body weight hang. She gasped at the strain as the muscles in her hands and shoulders instantly ached. But she had no time to wait.

Rebecca exited the tunnel and saw what was happening just as Sam swung her legs out over the drop.

“What are you doing?!” Rebecca cried out. “Come back! Please.”

But Sam was determined. She stared back at her sister with a mix of tears and steely resolve in her eyes. She grabbed a spring-loaded grapnel and thrust it into the crack ahead of her. Its arms expanded in the small fissure and fixed in place. She looped her rope into it, and almost immediately, it was able to take some of the weight from her.

Juno emerged beside Rebecca.

“Please, Sam. No!” Rebecca called out desperately.

But Juno’s attention was elsewhere because she’d heard a noise—not from behind them, but from somewhere in here.

Her torch scanned every surface. Then she saw it: a crawler, pale and monstrous, creeping along the ceiling like a twisted spider. It moved fast, skittering across the rock towards Sam from the other side of the gorge.

Sam saw it too, and her heart froze. She glanced back across the void at Rebecca, and their eyes met in a silent, devastating exchange. Because a sudden realisation had hit Sam: she wouldn’t make it back to the ledge in time. The distance she had already travelled was too great.

There was no hesitation in her next move. She held Rebecca’s gaze one moment longer before wedging a grapnel into the crack overhead, securing her safety line even more.

Then she pulled her clasp knife from its sheath, placed it between her teeth, and bit down on its handle, preparing for what she knew was her only viable option.

She had to fight.

Taking a breath, she gripped the fissure tighter, her

muscles burning from the strain. Then she moved hand over hand—not towards safety, but directly towards the oncoming beast.

"What are you doing?" Rebecca cried.

Sam hung from one hand as she grabbed the knife from her mouth. "I can get it," she called back. She stared down the creature hanging upside down in front of her, which reared up as it growled.

Sam had only one thing on her mind. She had to get rid of this thing if any of them were to survive. There was no other option. Her adrenaline pumped furiously and she felt like she might win this. She could win this.

But hanging above the gorge with only one free hand, all she managed to do was swing her knife wildly at the crawler, who easily avoided every swing.

It tilted its head curiously at her. Almost pitifully. Then, with a long-clawed hand, it lashed out with a single brutal swipe. Its talons tore through Sam's throat with a furious precision.

"No!" Rebecca screamed.

Sam's body immediately went limp, and her hand lost its grip on the ceiling. She fell backwards and dangled on the safety rope like a marionette, blood gushing from her throat and down into the gorge.

The creature hissed viciously, and it crawled closer.

Then Sam, with all the life she had left, lifted her legs and wrapped them around the crawler's back. She grabbed onto it tightly with her arms.

The blood poured from her neck, down her face, and

into her eyes, so she closed them tight as she gripped the knife and thrust it repeatedly into the creature's side. Straight into its heart.

Rebecca and Juno could only watch in horror.

The crawler screeched. It lost its grip on the ceiling and, with their combined weights, ripped the safety rope away from the first grapnel's mooring. They tumbled down together in a deathly embrace, but once the rope hit the second grapnel, it lurched Sam's body back. The creature wailed as it plummeted into the dark and crashed into the water below.

Sam was left hanging like a pendulum as her lifeless body swung back and forth on the safety rope.

Rebecca stood helplessly on the ledge, distraught in silent grief as she stared at her sister.

Juno, with one arm around her, turned Rebecca's gaze away from the corpse and towards herself. Rebecca's body went limp and she leaned against the wall, eyes still wide with shock as she stared at Juno. Silently pleading for help. For time to go back. For this to not be real.

"We can't stay here," Juno said urgently.

Rebecca just shook her head and said quietly, "Then go."

"No." Juno leaned forward and grabbed her shoulders. "We can still get out! We have to!"

"I don't care," Rebecca said. The tears came once more and upset gave way to anger. "What does it even matter? We're fucked. We were fucked the moment we set foot in this place. Every step we took... takes us closer... to hell!"

Neither had noticed that the monstrous noises in the

distance had stopped, that the masses of crawlers had still not caught them.

"I am not going to let us die in this hole!"

"Don't you understand?" Rebecca cried. "It's the cave. It won't let us leave! It won't let us—"

Rebecca's body was suddenly yanked backwards by a clawed hand that'd grabbed her ankle. When she landed face down on the rocky ledge, the air was immediately knocked out of her lungs.

"Becca!" Juno screamed, unable to do anything else before Rebecca was violently yanked backwards into the tunnel with a blood-curdling cry.

Chapter 13

ESCAPE

"Help me!" Rebecca screamed as she was dragged backwards into the narrow tunnel. Her fingers dug desperately into the dirt and jagged rock around her, breaking and scraping against the rough surface as she was ripped away.

Juno dropped her pick to the floor and lunged into the tunnel headfirst. She scrambled in and grabbed hold of Rebecca's bandaged hand. But the second Juno gripped tight to try to pull her back, the wound on Rebecca's hand burst open and she let out a scream of agony. The bandage slipped in Juno's grasp as the blood flowed out, forcing her to grip even tighter onto the raw injury.

"I've got you!" Juno shouted. Rebecca wailed in pain, and the talons dug into her ankle as they pulled and clawed at her from behind.

Juno swung her legs around and braced herself against the rock, pulling Rebecca's hand with all her might.

Screaming and kicking wildly, Rebecca tried to shake off the monster clinging to her, but her efforts did nothing. Its pull was unrelenting. Its roar was murderous. She cried out as she felt the claws rip deeper through her ankle, scraping the bone and slicing through nerves.

For a second, between the howls and cries, Rebecca's gaze met Juno's.

"Juno," she managed to say in a whimpered plea.

With a final, brutal tug, Rebecca was ripped out of Juno's grasp and dragged back into the darkness. The creatures were too strong. Rebecca's hand was too bloody.

"No!" Juno screamed in rage as Rebecca's cries faded away.

Backing out of the tunnel, Juno's hands trembled as she turned to look out over the gorge. Her headlamp flickered, casting its narrow beam upon Sam's lifeless body, swinging precariously on the safety rope. Blood still seeped from her neck, dripping into the dark below.

Her shaken gaze shifted to the frayed rope that barely supported Sam's weight, then across to the opposite ledge, just within the faint reach of her light.

Rebecca's words echoed in her mind. It's the cave. It won't let us leave. Staring at the ledges on either side and the maze of tunnels beyond, Juno could no longer disagree. It felt like a demonic labyrinth with no escape, designed to trap them forever—mocking them with false exits and misleading arrows.

The monstrous roars echoed again from the tunnel behind her, closer now. They were coming back.

There was no time. She had one choice—to jump. But not across, as the gap was far too wide. There was only one direction left. Down.

She knew they were coming for her.

She had no time, no other options.

The noise built louder and louder and the crawlers scrambled through the tunnel, clawing over each other to get to their next meal, to punish the next interloper in their home.

She retrieved her pick from the dirt and held it tightly to her chest. Closing her eyes, she accepted that this could be the end as much as it could be her escape. The water below could be shallow, enough to shatter her bones on impact, or it could be deep enough for her to land safely. Or she could collide with the creature that fell. Anything was better than being torn apart by the horrors coming at her.

With a final, quiet breath, Juno took a small step off the edge and silently plunged into the pitch black below.

Time slowed as the ground vanished beneath her feet. Her body cut through the thick air, weightless in the void while the wind howled around her. She clenched her jaw against the rush of air, tightening her body into a streamlined form, legs straight, toes pointed, like she could control her descent in some small way. There was no light aside from her weak, dying snap light on her jacket, illuminating nothing but the whirling abyss around her.

The roar of the creatures above fell away, and her mind latched onto the unknown.

She hoped that if the water was shallow, it would kill her quickly and spare her the pain of every bone shattering. But she held on to the smallest hope that maybe—just maybe—the water would be deep enough to save her.

Without another thought, her feet cut through the water and she sank at speed into a very deep pool.

Juno broke through the surface of the water with a loud gasp. The grime and blood that'd covered her was washed away. The snap light on her jacket glowed in the water, exposing the clear depths beneath.

Juno looked around with dazed relief as the impact had shaken her. The pool itself was entirely enclosed, with water that dripped and poured down from the walls around it. From one side, a small waterfall gushed steadily from a wide crack in the stone, dropping a dozen feet into the water below. On a portion of outcropped stone, the creature lay smashed into the rock.

Weak from exhaustion, Juno floundered while she tried to tread water. Her consciousness waned and her strength ebbed away.

"Juno!" came a familiar voice, snapping her awake.

Sarah leaned out of the waterfall fissure, holding a flaming torch that shone brightly over the water.

"Grab my hand!" she called out as she knelt and dangled a free hand towards her.

Using all her reserves, Juno swam over beneath the waterfall and clambered up onto the edge. After attaching her pick to her belt, she used both hands to climb. As she did, she stared up with a happy smile at her saviour.

Once she'd gotten closer, Sarah came more into view. Her hair was matted with filth and dishevelled across her face. Her clothes—what remained of them—were tattered and bloodied. Her bare arms and legs were stained with gore and covered with cuts and bruises. She looked every inch the primal warrior she had been forced to become.

"Thank you," Juno said. She climbed into the fissure and embraced her friend. But as she did, she felt the stickiness in Sarah's hair and could smell the odour of death all over her. Pulling back, Juno held her hands up and saw they were wet with blood. "Oh my god!" she said, and her expression morphed into worry. "What happened to you?" She glanced down and saw the large, bloodied bone held on Sarah's belt.

Sarah looked wearily into Juno's eyes. "I killed them," she muttered, then broke eye contact.

"Are you hurt?"

Sarah shook her head before looking back at Juno. "Rebecca? Sam?"

Juno could not bring herself to answer. A wave of grief flooded her mind with images of what she had gone through. She just shook her head mournfully.

Sarah's expression remained devoid of reaction. She just stared at Juno as she tilted her head. "What about Beth?"

"I'm so sorry," Juno mumbled. "She didn't make it."

"You saw her die?"

Juno didn't speak, just looked heartbroken.

"Did you?"

Juno swallowed and whispered, "Yes. I'm sorry."

Sarah stared at Juno and took a slow breath. Then, without another word, she turned to leave.

"Are you coming?" Her tone was flat and impatient.

"Did you find a way out?"

Sarah just walked on ahead, guiding them through the narrow fissure behind the waterfall and into a vast, shadowy cavern. Her torch flickered, casting a mix of yellow and orange light as they walked.

Without turning back, Sarah gestured towards a small backpack that rested on a large rock by the fissure's exit. "I found this."

Juno's heart raced. She recognised it—it was Holly's. Rushing over, she knelt beside the backpack. As her snap light illuminated its surface, she noticed the blood staining the fabric. She unzipped the pack, reached inside, and pulled out a couple of snap lights. Unclipping the dying one on her clothes, she quickly activated the new light with a crack. Its bright glow filled the dark in front of her. Then she pulled out a handful of flares. A small smile crept across her face and she retrieved her pack, unzipping it to reveal her own set of flares.

"We can use these," Juno said, counting them. "We got ten."

Sarah remained silent.

"Maybe we can distract those things."

Suddenly, shrieks echoed through the caverns behind them, piercing the stillness. Juno jumped to her feet, her heart racing. She finished stuffing Holly's flares into her rucksack and they both hurried deeper into the cave.

While Juno pressed on ahead, Sarah paused. She glanced down at Holly's abandoned pack and the pickaxe that was clipped to its side. She picked it up and hooked it onto her belt, letting the bone she had been using clatter to the floor.

Through the next set of caverns, Juno took the lead, guiding them both through narrow fissures, scrambling up inclines, and carefully stepping over jagged rocks. The silence between them was only broken by their laboured breathing and the occasional dripping of water that echoed off the cave walls.

The roars and wails that'd been in pursuit had stopped.

Reaching a fork in their path, Juno paused. Before stepping into one tunnel, she whipped out a flare from her bag, lit it, and tossed it as far down the left-hand tunnel as she could. It fizzed and hissed but bounced deeply in, its white glow sparkling up the dark.

"Hopefully, they'll follow that," Juno said, her voice tinged with uncertainty.

Sarah remained quiet, her expression still empty as she stared at Juno.

At each break in the path, Juno repeated this action—lighting a flare and throwing it down the route not chosen—hoping it could buy them enough time to find a safe route out.

Once they reached the base of an ascending passage, Sarah silently crept forward. Her flaming torch, though flickering as it neared the end of its life, still cast enough light to reveal their path ahead.

The passage up appeared empty. The cries of the monsters had still not returned.

"It's clear," Sarah whispered, her voice barely a breath. She raised her torch higher.

A soft breeze drifted down from the top of the passage, causing the fragile flame to flicker.

Juno followed cautiously, her open bag in hand. Her eyes constantly flicked over her shoulder, alert and tense, scanned the shadows behind them for any sign of movement.

Sarah motioned for her to take the lead again, which she willingly did. Her newly activated snap light provided enough of a glow to help her navigate the steep terrain while Sarah brought up the rear.

Partway up the incline, a nerve-shattering shriek sounded from behind them—close behind them.

They both froze.

Slowly glancing back, both Juno and Sarah searched the darkness. But all they could see was bare rock.

Whatever had made the noise remained unseen.

Feeling unsteady on the incline, Juno's eyes darted around, desperately scanning for some level ground or a place for them to hide. But there was nowhere to take cover. They were exposed on the steep slope.

Juno grabbed her last remaining flare and dropped her empty pack onto the rocky slant.

Another shriek sounded.

"Where are they?" Juno asked. "They're faster than us. They should be here!"

No sooner had the words left her mouth than another

shriek pierced the air, louder this time. But still, they could not see a single thing behind them.

"We need to move," Sarah said urgently.

Without hesitation, they turned and rushed up the slope and into the tunnel ahead, not wanting to wait any longer for the monsters.

They scrambled up winding, twisting passages, splashing through pools of gathered water, moving as fast as they could.

Behind them, in pursuit, the monstrous roars grew louder, reverberating through the tunnels, closing in on them.

Up the slope and down the tunnel they rushed. The breeze ahead of them grew stronger until they could feel it on their faces. As they turned a corner, Juno's question as to where the creatures were was answered.

At the end of the tunnel, four large crawlers crouched on the high rocks above their exit. Waiting for them. They made low clicking sounds as they stared at their prey, their heads tilting from side to side once they sensed their presence.

Striking up her last flare, Juno held it high. Its light hissed and fizzed brightly. Immediately, one of the crawlers launched from their rock straight towards Juno with incredible speed.

She only had time to take a step back and cry out before the creature slammed into her, knocking her backwards into a stream of stagnant liquid that lined one side of the tunnel.

Sarah's gaze did not leave the three other creatures

that waited up ahead. She held up her ebbing torch and screamed a guttural roar of defiance. Waving the flame at them like a weapon in front of her, she thrust it back and forth in desperation.

Behind her, Juno grappled with the attacking crawler. The muddied water around them splashed as their frenzied limbs thrashed. Juno grabbed the pick from her belt and desperately swung it at the crawler, cutting into its thigh.

Meanwhile, the three crawlers on the rocks had not been deterred by Sarah's flame and roars, and they crawled down onto the dirt floor in front of her. Their twisted, emaciated bodies crept closer on all fours, surrounding her. She grabbed Holly's pick from her belt and held it in her right hand, swapping her torch to her left.

She swung the torch towards them again, trying to ward them off. Two of the crawlers hesitated, momentarily retreating, unable to see her but still sensing the danger of her movement.

The third creature wasn't intimidated. With a low growl, it lunged, too fast for her to lift her pick.

The two women were locked in battle with the creatures. It was primal and savage, an unforgiving fight between two species, each determined to destroy the other.

With a snarl, Sarah swung her pick in a wide arc, burying it deep into the side of the first crawler's skull, killing it instantly. The sickening crunch echoed through the cavern.

Before she could react, the other two rushed her, slamming her to the ground with a force that knocked the torch from her grip.

Juno, meanwhile, was struggling. She sliced at the beast, but it clawed at her in return, and the stream below them started to turn red with the blood mixing into it. Both were ferocious, and Juno's adrenaline pushed her beyond any pain. As the claws cut open her side, she drove the pick into the crawler's chest, then its arm, then finally its jaw.

The sharp metal shattered its face, but the pick's handle splintered in her hands. Broken from such a forceful hit. The creature's body wilted and she screamed, enraged, pushing the beast off her. She grabbed it by the head and smashed its skull against the rocky ground. Its motionless body slumped into the dirty water.

Sarah still struggled, pinned beneath her two attackers, fighting like a cornered animal. Her movements were wild as she swung her pick, clawed with her hands, and kicked with every ounce of strength she had. But the crawlers on her were relentless, gouging and biting, their claws tearing through her skin.

One seized her by the throat and forced her face-down into the dirty stream. She thrashed violently as the crawler's grip tightened, and bubbles rose from her submerged face.

Juno, drenched and bloodied, stared as one crawler turned to her, leaving Sarah to be drowned. It roared and clambered over.

Grasping the remnants of her pick handle tightly, Juno gritted her teeth. And then, not waiting for the creature to make the first move, Juno lunged for the fallen torch, its flame almost out. She rolled to dodge the crawler's snapping jaw and flailing talons. It screamed after her.

Scrambling to her feet, she swung the flaming torch with everything she had. Missing, the crawler then barrelled at her. But as it opened its mouth wide, Juno thrust the torch forward.

It let out a deafening, inhuman cry as the flames burnt into its throat. The torch pushed deep into its mouth. Juno didn't hesitate and advanced on the crawler as it writhed backwards, and drove the jagged handle of her pick straight into its brain. The crawler's yelps turned to a choking gurgle before it fell with a thud.

Sarah, gasping for air as the crawler above her strangled her into the dirty stream, found a rock within reach. She grabbed it and catapulted it up rapidly. It smashed into the beast's head, sending it tumbling to one side. Then she straddled the dazed creature and used the full force of her might to smash the rock down onto its skull. With this one blow, the crawler's body spasmed and a wheezing death rattle escaped its lungs.

Then there was silence, besides Sarah's and Juno's laboured breaths and dripping water in the distance.

Sarah grabbed her pick from the bloody water and looked both ways up the tunnels. The headlamp on her helmet started to fade.

Juno couldn't help but smile in relief that they both stood. Victorious. She prayed that it was over, but when she turned to Sarah, she was met with a stare of pure hatred.

"You saw her die, you said."

Sarah's words were spoken through clenched teeth.

"Sarah, I—"

Sarah took a step forward. "She begged me to kill her, to stop them from coming to eat her alive."

Juno couldn't respond. She was frozen in fear. But not just in fear of Sarah, who stood there, bloodstained, pick in hand, with a hateful glare—because she also stood in fear of her own actions. Her own mistakes.

Sarah raised the pick, pointing it at Juno. "You. She told me what you did."

"It-It was an accident," Juno pleaded. "She came up behind me, and I turned and—"

"Not her!" Sarah bellowed so loudly that the echo around them amplified the sound to almost deafening proportions. "Him! What you did with him!"

Sarah reached up to a chain on her neck and pulled out the pendant.

Juno's heart clenched at the sight of it, her mind racing, piecing together what was happening.

Weakly, she replied, "I don't—"

She knew nothing could appease Sarah now. The only thing she could say still slipped out as a whimper.

"I'm sorry."

Sarah's chest heaved as anger pulsed through her, her breathing deep and loud—almost like one of those creatures—and she sized up her prey. "You—"

Except Juno's gaze was not on Sarah, but behind her.

Wide-eyed with her mouth open, she stared in terror at the far side of the cavern.

Turning, ripped from her hateful focus, Sarah saw what had caught Juno's attention. Across every surface—walls, ceiling, and floor—a veritable army of crawlers had crept up on them silently.

Sarah's fury had given their position away.

One creature at the front, paler and larger than the rest, reared up off its haunches and stood tall as it roared into the air, a rallying battle cry.

Juno turned in panic to escape. But all she saw was the pick in Sarah's hand swinging at her while she screamed just as animalistically as the crawlers had.

As if in slow motion, Juno stared helplessly at the arcing blade that careened through the air and collided with her knee. The metal sliced effortlessly through skin and muscle and into the bone itself. Lodging itself on impact.

There was no pain at first. Just a cold shock.

Her leg buckled and Juno collapsed. She did not hear the large number of crawlers advancing upon them. She only stared up at Sarah's face—twisting into a toothy, maniacal grin—before Sarah then broke off and ran in the other direction, away from the monsters. Deliberately leaving Juno behind.

Sarah just kept her eyes forward as she scrambled up the incline ahead. She did not turn when the angry and distraught screams erupted.

"Fuck you!" Juno yelled in pain before the seething mass of monsters quickly barrelled upon her. "Fuck you, too," she yelled at them, next, and she yanked the pick out of her knee with an agonising yell. Ready to use a weapon.

Her fight was futile, though. She was quickly swarmed upon, and her battle cries twisted into excruciating screams.

Chapter 14

THE DESCENT

Sarah ran as fast as she could, turning this way and that, following any crudely drawn arrows on the walls that she saw. Almost blindly scrambling through the dark as her fading headlamp barely lit her way. The noise of the crawlers was distant but ever-present, threatening to catch up.

But after turning into one tunnel with an arrow pointing the way, she reached halfway down before she saw another arrow pointed back again.

"No!" she yelled.

She ignored this arrow and took a step farther down the tunnel, and without any warning, the ground beneath her disappeared. Her body fell through to darkness.

She could not stop her drop, and she rolled down a steep, uneven funnel of rock. Smashing off the walls as she went, tumbling head over heels through thick cobwebs, screaming in fury and fear in equal measure. Her helmet then smashed into a jagged rock, splitting in two.

*

Sarah's body slammed onto the earthy floor of a huge, cavernous chamber. Larger than any other she had been in before.

She coughed and felt a stinging pain in her chest. Rolling onto her back, she raised a hand to her ribs. When she pressed lightly where the soreness came from, a renewed wave of agony quickly burnt through her.

The cries of the crawlers in pursuit sounded so far away that Sarah didn't silence her pained scream, and she struggled to climb to her feet.

When she peered up, light washed over her face. As she faced this brightness, her pained expression fell away. Her blood-smeared skin glowed pink in the light that spilled down from the top of this expanse.

Slowly, her gaze fell to the rest of the cavern. As her eyes adjusted to the light, she began to see bones. Human and animal. Not just a few piles of scattered remains but an overwhelming mass, stacked grotesquely against the wall, towering like the remnants of a forgotten tomb. It was made from the bones of thousands. Ribcages crushed under femurs, skulls with empty sockets, all brittle and impossibly white, stacked like a staircase that led up to the light above.

Scattered among the bones, covered in dust, were different items. Bits of clothing the bodies had worn when they died, frayed and torn yet still attached. Moccasins, shattered beads, mining suits, rusted tools, and even what looked like ceremonial feathers lay stiff and decayed, attached on leather bands around a few skulls.

Sarah's breath quickened, not from the sight of the dead but from the light that clawed at her attention.

A way out.

She bolted. Racing up the bones as fast as she could. Clawing at the remains to get purchase. She scaled the steep incline of the dead.

Towards the light, her eyes fixed and unwavering. Ignoring her agony.

From some overgrown weeds around the base of a high rock face, Sarah's hand burst outward, reaching wildly for purchase. Grasping at some foliage, she held on tight and pulled herself out of the cleft. Her lungs filled with a sting of fresh air that washed the stale death from inside of her.

She shielded her eyes as they adjusted to the brightness, and she scrambled forward into the bright sunshine of the elevated clearing.

Wavering, she looked out at the world before her as it unfurled in breathtaking contrast to the nightmare below. The harsh, cold stone was replaced by the verdant and warm embrace of nature.

Since they'd entered the cave, the weather had turned from autumnal gloom into this unseasonable summer.

Ahead, the tree line broke to reveal the Appalachian landscape, bathed in the golden light of a late afternoon sun. The peaks in the distance rolled across the horizon like a gentle wave. Their rich, forested slopes were cloaked in a kaleidoscope of greens, browns, and oranges.

Above her, the sky was a vast, dark blue, dotted with

soft, cotton-like clouds that drifted lazily by. The sun, low and warm, cast its honeyed glow over her, and the gentle breeze carried with it the scent of pine needles and wildflowers. The birds called to one another from the trees above.

How long was I down there? Sarah thought, struggling to control her breath. Her rib throbbed.

Before long, a clawing fear spread from behind her, as if the monsters would burst out of the rocks at any second. Baying for her blood.

Without a second thought, and despite having very little energy and being in a lot of pain, Sarah ran. Downhill she stumbled, barely managing not to trip over the wild brush or her own boots. She had no real idea where she was going, so she simply ran in the only direction she could think of.

Reaching an overgrown plateau, Sarah pushed her way through the undergrowth in a fevered state of pure desperation, convinced that behind her, razor talons would be slashing wildly, trying to rip into her legs.

But then, just as she broke through a thick section of brush and out onto a gravel road, Sarah found herself—by some miracle—running straight towards their vehicles.

Sarah slammed the key into the ignition and fired up the engine while laughing maniacally. Her eyes were wide and confused. Her grin was trembling.

After throwing the gear into reverse, she looked into the rear-view mirror and saw herself. Saw her bloodied, bruised face. Saw her gore-matted hair. Saw the pure terror in her eyes.

A movement in the overgrowth just beyond the passenger-side window forced her to stomp on the gas pedal. The vehicle's wheels spun wildly on the loose dirt before finally getting a grip. The car lurched backwards through the trees until the clearing opened behind her. Then she yanked the wheel, and the car was sent into a one-hundred-eighty-degree skid, turning her about-face to point forward.

With a possessed look, she cackled and slammed on the gas. The vehicle skidded away down the treacherous track, leaving the cave behind her in a cloud of dust and dirt.

It smashed its way through any branches that hung across her path. The four-by-four heaved wildly on the uneven surface, threatening to steal her control and hurtle her off the steep drop to the side. But Sarah didn't consider that. All she wanted was to get away.

A few minutes later, the vehicle sped off the track. With a high-pitched squeal as the brakes kicked in, the four-by-four whipped around a tight bend and flew onto the empty mountain highway.

The sun was setting ahead on this open road, and her panic finally began to subside as her resolve weakened. Tears welled in her eyes. Psychologically overwhelmed and physically battered, she could not hold up her walls any longer.

Having to slam on the brakes and stop the car in the middle of the road, she finally broke down. Sarah sobbed uncontrollably as she stared down at her hands. The blood that covered them. Blood from her, her friends, and creatures.

How would she explain this? How could she explain this?

The engine rumbled softly and Sarah slumped forward against the steering wheel.

Anger, remorse, guilt, fury, sorrow, grief, hate. They all collided with tremendous debilitation. She tried to breathe, but she could not grasp control, and the pain in her ribs burnt at her nerves. She only saw various images in her head.

A pick hitting Beth in the neck.

Jessica's small body crushed in the car.

Juno's scared face staring back at her.

Holly's bloodied scream as her flesh was ripped apart.

Juno and Paul kissing.

Flashes of memory and imagination collided with her thoughts. Reality and fiction blurred as her resolve fragmented and shattered.

She peered up through her tear-filled vision and saw in the mirror as a blurred shape hurtled towards her.

Before she had time to react, or even wipe the tears from her eyes, a large logging truck rocketed past the Jeep, honking its horn in protest at her in the middle of the road.

She screamed as her vehicle rocked, caught in the truck's wake.

Squeezing her eyes shut, Sarah tried with all her might to force this torment away. She knew she had to move. She knew she had to keep going.

She reached out to grab the gear stick to keep on

driving—but was suddenly met with the vengeful stare of Juno, who sat next to her in the passenger seat.

Across her face and body, wide, deep, fatal gouges bled profusely.

"You murdered us," she gargled as she raised a bloody pick.

With a jolt, Sarah's eyes snapped open. Her breathing came shallow and her body trembled. In the depths of the empty, cavernous chamber, the headlamp from her helmet lay on the floor beside her. Her helmet was not cracked, and the light still shone bright.

She glanced to her side, expecting to see a large tower of bones and, above it, the bright ray of beautiful sunlight leading to freedom.

But there was only darkness. Thick, cold darkness.

No bones. No exit.

She drew her legs in close, bringing her knees up to her chin. All emotion drained from her face, and she began to softly rock back and forth.

The pain in her chest had gone, but so had all the fear.

"Happy birthday, Jessie-bear," she said in a whisper. A loving smile crept over her face. "You're finally six today!"

"I love you so much, Mummy."

When Sarah opened her eyes, the cave was lit by the flickering glow of six birthday candles on a large cake.

Sitting on the rocky ground opposite her was Jessica, who was smiling back at her. "Can I open my presents now?"

"Of course you can," Sarah replied, lost in thought.

Everything was perfect.

Everything was as it had to be.

At the edges of the cavern, dozens upon dozens of the blind creatures had surrounded her. None of them advanced. None attacked. There came no shrieks nor growls.

They just stood in witness to this interloper.

Listening.

Waiting.

ABOUT THE AUTHOR

Christian Francis is an author specializing in the darkest of fantasy and the strangest of horror. Alongside his original works for both adult and YA audiences, he has penned official novelizations of classic genre films, including *Session 9*, *Maniac Cop* (1, 2, and 3), *The First Power*, *In The Mouth of Madness*, *The Gate*, and many more. Keep up to date with his latest work: echohorror.com